The Streets of Sundown

Hampered by a corrupt administration, the sheriff of Sundown really had a problem on his hands. The army forces at Fort Laramie had been whittled down and it soon became clear that little could be done to keep law and order among the frontier outposts. Gradually Sundown had acquired the reputation of a wild town, a hell of gambling halls and saloons, all run by corrupt men with a private army of hired gunslingers.

Then, one evening, a stranger appeared in Sundown, a man dressed in black who wore his guns low, a killer with a purpose. An hour later, two of the hired gunslingers lay dead in the dusty main street of Sundown.

For the first time the gamblers and crooked cattle barons discovered that they were faced by a man who knew no fear, whose gun was faster than those carried by their hirelings, and a man who took orders from no one. So long as that man remained alive and in Sundown, their very existence was threatened. All hell would break loose!

The Streets of Sundown

RICHARD D. HOWARD

A Black Horse Western

ROBERT HALE · LONDON

© 1962, 2002 John Glasby
First hardcover edition 2002
Originally published in paperback as
The Savage Gun by Chuck Adams

ISBN 0 7090 7208 2

Robert Hale Limited
Clerkenwell House
Clerkenwell Green
London EC1R 0HT

Typeset by
Derek Doyle & Associates, Liverpool.
Printed and bound in Great Britain by
Antony Rowe Limited, Wiltshire

1

Gun Law

Long before daylight, Bret Manders was in the saddle, heading west into a vast, empty stillness which lay over the sullen land like a shadow. For an hour, there was no sound but the continual drum of hoofbeats on the hard ground. The sun came up, promised to bring a hot day to the parched, arid desert which stretched in from of him as far as the eye could see. He had left the timber line a little before evening on the previous day. Fifteen miles away lay the frontier town of Sundown – and vengeance.

By midday, he was crossing the desert in a steady lope, sorely tempted to dismount and rest up a while but there was the pressing need to reach the far edge of the desert before nightfall and this kept him in the saddle. In the sweltering heat and dull, endless monotony of the desert, he missed the green freshness of the vegetation which he had left behind him.

He sat easily in the saddle, a tall, hawk-faced man dressed completely in black, carrying his guns low on his hips: a broad-shouldered man with the build of an athlete and the blue, ice-chip eyes of a born killer. There was no star beneath the black jacket and the lawmen of a score of frontier towns would have given their eye teeth for a chance to get him at the wrong end of a gun. The notches on his gun told of ten men dead, but the hard expression on his face told of more to come.

Suddenly, crossing the crest of a low ridge, the stallion suddenly flicked its ears and whinnied sharply. A second later, there was a brief blossoming of white smoke from a clump of gnarled hackberry trees and in that same moment, with a swiftness born of instinctive reflexes, he had hurled himself out of the saddle, hitting the hard ground with a bone-jarring blow and rolling over once before coming lithely to his feet, his heavy Colt balanced in his right hand. The bullet ripped viciously through the air where his head had been a moment earlier and ricocheted off the rocks behind him. Swiftly, he began to move away from the stallion. There was no need to tether him; the horse would remain standing there until he whistled; there was perfect understanding between the two of them. He reached another low rise, lifted his head cautiously and found himself looking down into a long hollow, flanked by high ridges on either side. A sudden movement caught his keen gaze a hundred yards or so to his left among the hackberry trees. Whoever had tried to bushwhack him was still there, not sure whether his bullet had found its mark, and not keen on taking any chances. With the trained eye of a frontiersman, he watched his adversary moving swiftly from cover to cover as the other worked his way around in a wide circle, obviously with the intention of coming up on him from the flank.

Bret smiled grimly to himself. With the ease and stealth of an Indian scout, he wriggled back between the rising columns of rock, taking advantage of every scrap of cover, making no sound, gradually moving towards a tall heap of boulders which overlooked the narrow trail along which the other would come. Here, under the blazing noonday sun with few shadows, the ground dipped and rose several times and he paused often to survey the position before he crawled on, his mind and body alert and prepared.

Without the faintest whisper of sound, he reached his

place of concealment and lay waiting. The other man was clearly not as versed as he was in the ways of tracking down a quarry for he made plenty of noise as he edged his way forward along the narrow trail. Bret waited patiently until the other had drawn level with his hiding place, waited for another five seconds, then rose lithely and silently to his feet, the barrel of the Colt trained on the other man's back.

Then he said, very quietly and calmly: 'Just take it easy, mister, and drop that rifle. I'm not looking for trouble right now, but if you ask for it, you'll get it.'

He heard the audible hiss of astonishment as the other drew in a sharp breath, then the rifle clattered loudly on to the rocks and the man drew himself up to his full height, raising his hands slowly above his head.

'That's better.' Bret moved forward, cautiously, but with every movement calm and unhurried. 'Now turn round so's I can get a better look at you.'

Very slowly, the other turned to face him. The man was tall and singularly thin, and the buckskin hunting shirt seemed to hang on his spare frame. The hair that showed beneath the wide-brimmed hat was sparse and grey, the ends bleached by the sun. On the face of it, Bret decided, he didn't look like a killer, but you could never tell.

The man eyed him steadily for a few moments, then shrugged his shoulders with a peculiarly resigned motion. 'Go ahead, killer!' he snarled. 'Why don't you shoot me and get it over with. I ain't goin' to plead with you.'

'I don't want to kill you, but I'd sure like to know why you tried to kill me.' Bret regarded the other closely, even critically. He holstered his gun, certain now that there would be no more trouble from the other. The man looked perplexed, eyed the gun in Bret's holster for a brief second, then looked up, his gaze flicking back to Bret's face He had been scared of him at first, but now he seemed to have regained control of himself and was facing him with a new-found courage and determination.

'I mistook you for one of those hired gunslingers from Sundown. I guess I must have been wrong, mister.' His eyes narrowed suspiciously, as he stared hard at Bret. 'But you're dressed all in black and I don't see any marshal's star.'

'You won't.' Bret whistled shrilly for the stallion. 'I'm no lawman. I'll accept that you only meant to kill me because you thought I was a hired killer. Just who is it that's doing the hiring around these parts?'

The stallion whinnied softly as it came up to him. Leaning against one of the pillars of rock, Bret took paper and tobacco from his pocket and began to roll himself a cigarette. Not once did the steely blue eyes leave the other man's face.

'You must be a stranger in these parts, mister, if you ain't heard of Darby Wicker. He runs the town of Sundown across the desert there. Either you go in with him, or you don't live long. It ain't healthy to set yourself agin him.'

'Wicker.' Bret nodded, drew on the cigarette. 'Seems I've heard that name somewheres before.'

'He was in the Confederate Army during the war,' went on the other. 'I guess the fighting got into his blood. Didn't want to stop when it was all over. When the others laid down their arms, accepted the constitution, he moved west, came out here a couple of years ago. Started buying up most of the good ranch-land in these parts, then moved into Sundown. Set up saloons, half a dozen gambling joints. Hired himself a private army of gunslingers. They rustle our cattle, slaughter those they don't take away, burn our ranches, pull down our fences. Pretty soon, they'll drive us all clear out of the state.'

'So?' said Bret thoughtfully, 'And what's the law doin' about it all? Is there no sheriff in Sundown?'

'There is. Seth Veldon, But he's an old man pushin' sixty. He daren't raise a gun against these killers, not if he values his life.' There was disgust in the other's harsh voice. He spat into the sand. 'You see, mister, there ain't no law around here except Darby Wicker. He gives the orders and everybody jumps to 'em. You ride into Sundown and you'd better do the same if you want to keep yore hide whole.'

Bret finished his cigarette, flicked it into the brush. 'Might take a ride into town at that, seeing I'm heading that way. I'd like to meet this Darby Wicker face to face.' The steely glint in his clear blue eyes belied the faint sardonic amusement in his voice. 'Could be he's the man I've been looking for.'

'You aimin' on tying in with that bunch of outlaws?' snarled the other, almost exploding with anger. 'If'n you are, I reckon I ought to have shot you when I had the chance.'

Bret shook his head slowly. 'You never had the chance,' he said meaningly. 'But don't get me wrong. I don't aim to team up with Wicker. If he is the *hombre* I'm looking for, even his private army of gunhawks won't save him. I promise you that.'

Smoothly, he swung himself up into the saddle, sat easily, glancing down at the other, at the sudden, surprised expression on the old man's face as he stooped to pick up the fallen rifle. Bret saw with a quick glance that it was a brand new Winchester. 'Better get your mount and ride back the way you came,' he advised quietly. 'This isn't going to be any concern of yours.'

'Mebbe you're a big man, mister, and a fast man with the draw, but you can't set yourself up against the whole of Sundown and hope to come out of there alive.'

'Perhaps.' There was something cruel about the smile on the thin lips. 'But like I just said, that ain't no concern of yours.'

He touched spurs to the stallion, rode along the dusty trail, down into the valley below. Not once did he look back as the other stared after him for a few moments, then climbed slowly into the saddle.

*

As Bret rode slowly along the narrow, dusty trail which wound across the flat desert, he quartered the horizon keenly, slitting his eyes against the harsh glare of the sunlight which shocked up from the desert in dizzying waves of heat. To his right, the low foothills petered out gradually into a flat mesa which stretched away apparently endlessly to the misted horizon where the tall range of mountains undulated at the far extent of his vision.

To his left, nearer at hand, the desert ended more abruptly and there was a rich cattle spread on the far side of a sluggish river. The welcome touch of greenness brought a refreshing feel to his gaze which seemed to have looked far too long upon the dry, yellow face of the desert. Now that the sun was westering slowly, the shadows were lengthening and he realized that whoever had taken that spread just across the river, had chosen the spot well. It was the first patch of grassland for close on fifteen miles and watered as it was by the river, it would undoubtedly give a good yield of grazing fodder for cattle.

He touched spur to the horse, wheeled towards the smoothly flowing river as something caught his eye. There was, he thought, something definitely sinister about that faint haze of smoke which appeared above the spur of high ground in the distance. Swiftly, he breasted the rise and found himself looking down on a smooth stretch of grassland which lay between him and what had once been a proud and beautiful ranch house. Now, it was little more than a smouldering heap of ashes, of burning uprights and resinous flame.

Reaching the scene of destruction, he slid swiftly from the saddle, went forward on foot, partly-burnt lengths of wood snapping loudly under his feet. There was the sharply acrid smell of smoke stinging the back of his nostrils. Whoever had fired this place had certainly made an excellent job of it, he thought wryly. His keen eyes took in every detail, the smouldering timbers, the furniture which had been so badly ravaged by the flames that little of it was still recognizable. Clearly, this was not the work of any of the Indian tribes in the area, all of whom were at peace with the white settlers.

Diligently, he searched through the ruins for any sign of life. In one of the barns outside, he came across two horses. Both were dead and at first sight they seemed to have been suffocated by the dense smoke which must have been produced by the smouldering, wet fodder. Then he looked a little more closely and saw to his surprise that they had both been shot carefully through the head at close range. Examining them closely, he failed to hear the slow but cat-footed tread and his first inkling of danger, one which sent his right hand striking for the gun at his belt, was the sharp whinny of the stallion tethered to the rail outside the burnt-out shell of the ranch house. He whirled, but not quite quickly enough. The man who held the short-barrelled rifle, pointed straight at his chest, was of middle age. Once, he had undoubtedly been a fine-looking man, but not now. He swayed uncertainly as he stood there, holding the rifle in one hand, propping himself up with the other. Both eyes were swollen so as to be almost completely closed. The bruised flesh on his cheeks had turned an angry shade of mottled purple and both lips were puffed out to twice their normal size. There was blood on the left sleeve of his shirt and the shape of his face seemed to have been distorted. Either his jaw had been dislocated, or was perhaps even broken.

Whatever the cause, when he spoke, his voice was little more than a husky whisper which came out painfully through the swollen lips and he was obviously in great pain whenever he formed the words.

'I'm going to kill you, you thieving, murdering gun-hawk,' he whispered thinly. 'And you aren't goin' to die easy. This is the last time you go around burning the ranches of peaceful citizens.'

'Now just a minute,' interrupted Bret quickly. Even though the other had been badly beaten up, was almost out on his feet, the hand which held the short rifle, tucked under the arm, was quite steady and he looked like a man who had been driven by circumstances far beyond the limit of human endurance, one who would not hesitate to press the trigger without listening to any explanations.

'Don't try to soft-talk me, mister,' croaked the other indistinctly. 'I don't know why you decided to stay behind when the others left, but it sure wasn't for the benefit of my health. Mebbe you thought there might be money around some place and you just came back to try to find it.'

Bret shook his head slowly, keeping his hand well away from the gun at his waist. 'You've got it all wrong, old-timer,' he said quietly, unhurriedly. 'And before you do anything foolish, I think you ought to hear what I have to say. I reckon I can guess what happened here. This is some of Darby Wicker's work.'

'Yeah, as if you didn't know.'

Through narrowed eyes, Bret saw the other's knuckles as his fingers tightened around the butt of the rifle and across the trigger. The look on the man's face told him that he didn't believe what he was trying to tell him, that he intended to shoot and take no chances. Swiftly, he judged the distance between them, knew instinctively that he had no chance to cover that distance before the other, even in his present condition, pressed that trigger; that he did not even have a fighting chance of drawing on him and shooting the rifle out of his hands.

'I've heard the story about Darby Wicker from a rancher I met along the desert trail a couple of hours ago,' said Bret quickly, watching the other's face. 'That's one of the reasons I'm here. I, too, have a score to settle with him and neither you, nor any of his hired gunslingers, are going to stop me.'

For the first time, he saw the other hesitate and knew that he had the advantage. He went on swiftly. 'It's my guess that he tried to buy you out and you refused his offer. Now, he's sent in his killers to smoke you out.' He turned his head slowly to take in the smouldering devastation. 'But you weren't scared so easy. You thought that you could stand them off, so you fought it out with them. That's why they burned down your ranch, killed your horses, probably stampeded your cattle, left you for dead. Am I right?'

The other went to nod his head but the terrible agony on his face stopped him in a single instant and beads of perspiration stood out on his face and neck. He lowered the rifle reluctantly, clinging to the side of the barn for support. Bret gave a quick nod. 'That's better, *amigo*,' he said quietly. 'Now I think I should take a look at that face of yours. They seem to have given you a bad time.'

Holding the old man by the arm he led him away from the barn, out into the open, made him sit beside the well which had been sunk in the courtyard in front of the ranch. He had very few instruments with which to work and water from the well had to be boiled over a small fire which was easily lit with the burning pieces of wood from the ranch house. The other sat with his back against the stone wall of the well and watched him out of lack-lustre eyes.

'Looks like a bullet wound in your arm,' said Bret conversationally. 'I'd better take a look at that as soon as I've seen to your jaw. This isn't going to be pleasant.'

'You don't need to worry about me, stranger,' said the other. 'I ain't looking forward to it, but somehow, I've got the feeling you're a man who can be trusted.'

'Perhaps. I'm not a qualified surgeon, but I've taken out a dozen bullets or so in my time and when you ride alone like I do, you have to know a little about doctoring.' He rose to his feet, slipped his knife into the pan of boiling water until it completely covered the long, slender, well-honed blade, then stood close behind the other, holding his face gently in both hands. 'This is going to hurt like hell,' he said softly.

'Go ahead. I can take it,' gritted the other. Beads of perspiration stood out on his forehead as Bret suddenly tightened his grip. His smoothly probing fingers had detected the dislocation of the jawbone and he sucked in his breath sharply, then pressed smoothly, but quickly. The other gave a quick, sharp gasp of agony, then slumped against him. For a moment, Bret thought that the other had fainted and would have been grateful if that had been the case, but a second later the other's eyes flickered open, he gave a shuddering gasp, then felt his cheeks tenderly.

Bret's mouth twisted into a wry grin. 'Think you can still take any probing for that bullet, old-timer?' he asked tightly.

'You go ahead and git it out,' grated the other, speaking with difficulty. 'Once you've finished, I've got work to do.'

Bret walked over to the pan where the water was still boiling away, sterilizing the blade of the knife. In the circumstances, this was the best he could do. How deeply the bullet was embedded in the other's arm, it was difficult to tell from a superficial examination, but he guessed that it had not chipped the bone. He might have to probe for it for some time, though, and he did not want to run the risk of any infection getting into the wound.

He turned his head slowly, taking the knife from the pan. 'If you've got any ideas of going after those killers, I'd forget them,' he said firmly. 'From what I've heard, there are more hired gunslingers in Sundown than decent citizens. You'd be shot dead as soon as you set foot in the town.'

Very carefully, he probed for the bullet, grateful for the medical training which was sufficient for him to get out slugs and treat minor injuries. The other gritted his teeth, even though that effort must have cost him a lot of pain, and twisted his features into a grimace of agony. Bret found the bullet at last, lodged against the bone in the other's upper arm. Gently, he eased it out and plugged the wound, binding it with clean strips of cloth. He gave the other a brief nod of encouragement. 'That should do it. Better give it all the rest you can. Do you have any neighbours where you can rest up for a while?'

'Very few. There aren't many left now,' said the other bitterly. 'Wicker has been very thorough. Nobody seems to have the guts to stand up to him. 'There is no law in this country now but gun-law and he has everything on his side.'

'Sundown sounds like a fine town.' Bret's lips curled into a faint sneer. 'I still reckon you should go to someone you can trust, even if only for a few weeks. By the end of that time, either this place will be fit to live in again, or—' He paused deliberately.

'Or what?' queried the other, flexing his arm experimentally.

'Or I shall be dead,' finished Bret quietly. 'You see, I too, have a score to settle with Darby Wicker.' He helped the other to his feet, threw a swift glance at the ruined homestead, tightened his lips into a grimace of deep anger, then whistled for the stallion. The other stood watching him closely, then gave a brief nod. His face no longer had the colour of putty and some of the colour had come back to his cheeks. Bret felt satisfied with the surgical job he had carried out. The wound was clean and he doubted if there would be any infection.

Darby Wicker came out into the main street of Sundown and looked down towards the sheriff's office. There were few people on the wooden sidewalks at that hour of the early afternoon, with the blazing heat of the sun burning on to the dust. A handful of horses champed hungrily at their bits, tethered to the hitching rails outside the saloon. A couple of men sat with their backs and shoulders against the wooden wall of the livery stable, their broad-brimmed hats pulled low over their eyes, drowsing in what little shade they could find.

Pulling his lips together into a thin, cruel gash, he strode along the narrow street, climbed up on to the wooden sidewalk and made his way quickly towards the sheriff's office. Reaching the door, he flung it open and stormed inside.

'Veldon,' he yelled harshly. 'Get in here.'

A short, stocky figure came into the room through the far doorway. The sheriff stood for a moment looking across at Wicker, then his shoulders sagged a little, almost imperceptibly, but the gesture was not lost on the man who faced him. He said in a faintly faltering voice: 'I guess you've come about McKay, Mr Wicker.'

'That's right. I've warned you before, Veldon, that I give the orders around here and I won't stand for any of my men being thrown into this jail unless I give the say-so. I reckon you'd better let him out right now.'

'You know I can't do that,' persisted the other thinly. He came forward a couple of paces, but not once did he lift his eyes to look directly at the other. 'He shot two men down in the street last night and I've got to hold him fer trial. If it was self-defence as he claims, then he'll get off. But that's up to a jury.'

Wicker's voice dropped to a faintly purring note. 'You know as well as I do, Sheriff—' he began, and there was a sneering touch to his voice as he gave the other his title; '—that those two ranch hands fired first. There are six witnesses to that. Now get him out, pronto, or do I have to get a new sheriff for Sundown?' There was no mistaking the threat in his silky voice.

For a moment longer, the sheriff hesitated, then he shrugged his shoulders resignedly and reached for the bunch of keys on the wall behind him. 'Very well, Mr Wicker,' he sighed. 'I'll get him. But there'll be trouble. The ranchers won't stand for this much longer, having their men shot down in cold blood in the street and then letting their murderers go free like this. Believe me —'

'Shut up, you stinking rat,' Wicker snarled at him. With

a deceiving slowness, he pulled the thick, bullhide whip from his belt, lashed at the other as he stumbled, turning for the door. There was a vicious twist to his lips.

The sheriff half-fell against the door, then pulled himself swiftly upright and vanished along the narrow passage. Wicker stood waiting beside the table, coiling and uncoiling the whip in his hands. There came the sound of metal grating on metal, the hollow clang of a heavy door being opened and then shut. When the sheriff returned, there was another man close on his heels. A tall, thin-faced man, obviously a half-breed, with an empty gun-belt at his waist.

'Get his guns, Sheriff,' said Wicker meaningly.

There was a thin, sneering smile on the half-breed's face as Veldon unhooked the guns which had been hanging from their trigger guards on nails on the wall behind the desk and handed them over to him. Still grinning, he holstered them and leered at the sheriff.

'Next time you try to take them away from me, I'll shoot you where you stand. Don't ever forget that,' he said thickly.

The other was about to protest, when the half-breed struck him across the mouth with his clenched fist. Staggering back, the sheriff fell against the corner of the desk, hung there for a moment with an expression of pain on his fleshy features, before sliding down on to the floor at the half-breed's feet.

As the other bent, fingers clutching at his shirt, to haul him back on to his feet, Wicker stopped him. 'Leave him now,' he ordered swiftly. The smile was back on his face. 'After all, we still need a sheriff here, if only for appearances sake. Get the rest of the boys together. We have to pay another call tonight. Things are happening far too slowly for my liking.'

'Sure, boss.' McKay released his hold on the sheriff, laughed thinly and harshly as the other fell back, striking his head against the leg of the table. 'Mebbe we ought to get permission from the sheriff. Or perhaps we could get him to come with us, to make sure that justice is done.'

After they had gone, closing the street door quietly behind them, Sheriff Veldon pulled himself painfully and unsteadily to his feet and sank down into the chair behind the table. His lips hurt where the half-breed's bunched fist had hammered into them. Deep down inside, he felt a despairing sense of futility, the sickening knowledge that he was merely a pawn in the big game that Darby Wicker was playing in Sundown. There was no law and order here, he reflected wearily, and never would be until someone came who dared to stand up to the other and his army of gunhawks. He poured himself a glass of wine, downed it in a single gulp. In fear of Wicker's vengeance, none of the townsfolk or the ranchers in the territory around Sundown, would dare to lift a hand against him. There was no law in this territory but gun-law. Wicker ought to have been hanged many months ago, but there had been no one strong enough, no one powerful enough, to do it and now things had got so completely out of hand, that Wicker had been able to establish himself as the big boss. He poured himself another drink and sipped it absently.

Outside, he could hear the raucous laughter which came from the direction of the saloon and knew what it meant. The gunhawks were gathering to strike once more. Some other rancher would have stubbornly refused to sell out to Wicker and for that, his ranch would be burned to the ground, his cattle driven off, and anyone who tried to shoot it out would be gunned down mercilessly. The homesteaders, too, were not immune to the violence. Their wheat and oat fields would be put to the torch, a whole year's hard labour would be wiped out in a single night.

Getting slowly to his feet, he walked to the window and stared moodily along the street. Even as he watched, he saw the half-breed, McKay, enter the saloon. There was no sign of Wicker and he guessed that the other had gone back to his own ranch, just outside of Sundown, to make preparations for the coming night.

The weariness settled over him more heavily. Three times he had tried to telegraph to the Rangers for help, but there had been no reply and as the days had lengthened into weeks, he had been forced to accept the inescapable fact that no help would ever be forthcoming, that the messages had either never been sent, or they had been stopped somehow by Wicker's men. He guessed that the operator in the telegraph office was in Wicker's pay. Twisting his lips into a grimace, he watched as a crowd of men poured out of the saloon, laughing and shouting, saddling their horses. Wicker's men. Getting ready to plunder and murder again. He wondered vaguely where the other had managed to find such men. There were always a few escaping from the law, moving west whenever things got a little too hot for comfort in the states back east; men who lived by the gun, who accepted no law and order, who knew that they had little to live for and were willing to fall in with any rich, powerful and unscrupulous man who offered them protection from the law and good pay in return for murder.

After they had ridden off, the street lay silent in the afternoon sun. The heat haze shivered towards the far end of town where the desert stretched away to the east. Once or twice, in the past, he had entertained ideas of saddling his horse and riding out there as far and as fast as he could go. But the sure knowledge that Wicker would send his men after him, had always stopped him. He had been forced to face the fact that he was a coward, too fond of his own skin to take that chance.

Buckling on his gunbelt, he went out into the street. There was a quietness over the town that he didn't like, it was as if a thunderstorm were building up on the horizon, ready to break at any minute, but the sky was clear, the sun hot on his back, and he tried to tell himself that it was nothing more than his imagination that was making him feel nervous.

Pushing open the batwing doors of the saloon, he went inside. There were a few men drinking at the bar and others seated around the tables in the middle of the room. One or two bore the stamp of Wicker's men and he felt a little shiver of tension run through him as he watched them eyeing him speculatively. He wondered for a moment what orders Wicker had given to them. Obviously they were to remain behind in Sundown, to watch out for any sign of trouble. It was an uneasy empire that Wicker ruled over, one which could, if the force of fear were lifted for a moment, if his iron rule faltered, blow up in his face. The townsfolk knew him for what he was, a ruthless killer. But they would try nothing so long as there were any of his gunmen around in the town.

'Trouble, Sheriff'?' asked the barman softly.

'Nope.' Veldon shook his head. 'Everything seems quiet enough.' He took the drink which the other pushed across the counter to him, downed it swiftly.

'Thought I saw Wicker going into your office a little while back,' went on the other softly. 'Saw him come out with that half-breed killer.'

In spite of himself. Veldon glanced nervously over his shoulder, but none of the men at the tables seemed to have heard. 'Couldn't hold him without any proper evidence,' he said defensively. 'Wicker had plenty of witnesses who would have sworn that McKay acted in self-defence.'

The other looked at him incredulously. 'Now you know that ain't true, Sheriff,' he said thinly, not raising his voice. 'I saw it happen myself. He shot them both down in cold blood. They never had a fair chance to go for their guns.'

Veldon looked at him hard. 'Better not go around talking like that if you want to stay healthy,' he said warningly, aware now that some heads were turned in their direction. 'It'd be your word against six or seven others.'

The barman moved his feet uncomfortably, staring over

Veldon's shoulder. In the mirror behind the bar, the sheriff saw that two of the men had risen to their feet and were walking slowly and softly towards him. They came up on either side of him, leaning on the bar. One of them said: 'You figgerin' on making trouble, Henders?' The dark eyes narrowed viciously. 'Sounded too much like you were accusin' McKay of murder.'

The other swallowed hard, his Adam's apple bobbing nervously in his throat. 'I didn't mean nuthin' like that,' he said, almost pleadingly, turning to the sheriff. 'Mebbe I saw wrong.'

'Mebbe you did,' sneered the other. 'But you talk too much. Mr Wicker doesn't like men who go around callin' his men murderers.'

'Take it easy,' interrupted Veldon quietly. 'He meant nothin'.'

'Mebbe not,' snarled the other. 'But you'd better keep out of this, Sheriff, unless you want more trouble with Wicker.'

'I'm not looking for trouble,' declared Veldon stoutly. 'But there has to be some form of law and order around here and as sheriff—'

'You're only sheriff because of Wicker's say-so,' said the man on the other side of him. 'Now keep your nose out of this. We're aimin' to teach this fella a lesson he won't fergit in a hurry.' Reaching over the bar, he grabbed a handful of the man's shirt, pulled him close. 'Now git from around there and out into the street,' he hissed warningly. 'Otherwise, I'll shoot you right there.'

White-faced, the barman worked his way around the back of the bar, his eyes never once leaving the gunman's face. Pushing up the wooden flap at the end, he stepped through, lowering it behind him.

'That's better,' grinned the gunhawk. He raised his voice so that everyone in the saloon could hear him. 'Now let's take him outside and see how well he can dance when we provide the music.'

Swiftly, the gun held on him, the barman scuttled towards the doors, pushed them open, and half-fell down the steps into the dusty street. A roar of raucous laughter bellowed from inside the saloon as the rest of the men piled out to watch the fun, knowing what was coming. Sick to his stomach, Sheriff Veldon stayed behind at the bar, but the second gunhawk, glancing back, said threateningly: 'Reckon you'd better come too, Sheriff. Just to see that nobody steps outside of the law.' He backed up his words with the six-gun which he held negligently, but menacingly, in his right hand.

Unwillingly, Veldon stepped out into the street, blinking his eyes against the harsh glare of the sunlight. The bar man stood in the middle of the street, looking wildly about him. His body jerked convulsively as the first shot bit into the dust at his feet. The gunman stood on the sidewalk, firing again and again, laughing at the top of his voice as the barman danced desperately from one foot to another as the bullets whined and ricocheted along the deserted street. Veldon stood by helplessly, knowing that as sheriff it was his duty to step in and put a stop to this act of lawlessness, but that he had only to make such a move for the men to turn on him. They might shoot him down where he stood. Or more likely still, they would stand him out there with the poor, unfortunate barman and make him dance ludicrously in the middle of the street.

'Dance!' shouted the bearded gunhawk loudly. 'Mebbe after this you'll—'

It said something for their concentration on the scene being enacted in front of them that no one had heard the quiet approach of the man who had ridden along the empty street into Sundown. But the quiet voice bit through the air like the lash of a whip, shearing off all sound.

'Better put up that gun, mister, if you want to stay alive!'

Stunned almost, shocked by the quiet, cold authority in the voice, Veldon whirled. The stranger, dressed completely in black, sat easily astride the magnificent stallion, eyes cold and hard. His hands rested loosely on the pommel of the saddle, well away from the guns which hung low on his hips.

The gunhawk's eyes narrowed viciously. The stranger's face was as expressionless as a mask. But the eyes, slitted beneath the broad-brimmed hat, were watchful and alert, waiting for the first hostile move from the men facing him.

Sheriff Veldon, watching from the shadows of the sidewalk, had the sudden, strange feeling that even though the odds were stacked against him, they were in favour of the man who sat easily astride the stallion, that he had somehow, taken over complete mastery of the situation.

'Seems to me you enjoy shooting up helpless men,' said the smooth voice. 'Mebbe you'd like to try it with me?'

For a long moment, the two men stood motionless, paralysed by fear, even though they both held their guns in their hands, and the stranger still had his holstered. There had been something in that calm, quiet voice which seemed to have filled both men with a strange kind of inertia. Then, the one with the beard seemed to stir himself, began moving very slowly, but with a deadly purpose, to the right, into the centre of the street, towards the trembling figure of the barman. Their strategy was obvious. They would attack the man from two sides and in spite of the calm authority in his voice, Veldon knew that none of the men on the sidewalk would make a move to help him if it came to a showdown.

The climax, when it came, was startling and sudden. Both gunhawks moved as one, bringing up their guns in the same instant. They were swinging level when with a swiftness that was too much to be followed by the eye, the stranger plucked both of his guns from their holsters and fired from the hip. To the watching crowd, it was as if the man on the horse had not moved. He fired with a peculiar disinterestedness, without a twitch of his facial muscles. A look, oddly like astonishment, spread over the bearded man's features as the gun dropped into the dust from his nerveless fingers. For an instant, there was a narrowing of his eyes as his body arched backward, then his knees sagged and he slumped into the dust.

The second man lay slumped against the hitching rail in front of the saloon, the small hole between his eyes just visible. The stranger eased his mount forward, holstering his guns. His keen gaze swept over the people gathered on the sidewalk. 'Anybody else want to make trouble?' he enquired, almost pleasantly, in a voice loud enough for everyone to hear. 'If they do, they can go for their irons right now.'

Nobody moved. The barman moved forward hesitantly. He spoke up harshly: 'Thanks, mister. But that was a foolish thing you did back there, killing those two men. Once Darby Wicker hears about this, he'll send his men gunning for yuh. Better stay on your horse and ride outa here as fast as you can. Sundown ain't goin' to be healthy for yuh from now on.'

'Darby Wicker. Seems I've heard that name somewheres before,' drawled Bret Manders. 'A mighty big man in these parts.'

'Too big for any one man to tangle with,' said Sheriff Veldon, stepping forward.

Bret eyed the star on the other's shirt. He said: 'If you're the sheriff in Sundown, how come you allow this lawlessness to go on'?'

Veldon shrugged. 'You don't know Wicker, stranger, or you wouldn't ask a question like that. He's the only law around these parts. These are two of his army of hired killers.' He nodded towards the dead men, 'He won't take kindly towards this.'

The crowd stood still in silence. 'Better do like the sheriff says,' said the barman, edging forward. 'Wicker will kill you when he finds out about this. There's been too much gunplay here.'

Bret nodded. 'I came here for a purpose,' he said

briskly. 'And I don't aim to leave, until I've finished what I set out to do.' He slid easily out of the saddle and hitched the stallion to the rail. Turning, he said softly: 'It seems to me that the good, decent people in Sundown outnumber the jackals that are riding with Wicker. Why are you so yellow-livered that you stand around and allow two gunmen to shoot up an innocent man just for sport.'

For a few moments no one moved, no one spoke. As one man they stared at the two dead men lying in the dust. Then, at the top of the steps, the crowd parted and a tall, slender woman came forward. Long, dark hair curled over her bare shoulders and her face bore a look of almost cynical amusement.

'What they're trying to tell you, stranger,' she said in a musical voice, 'is that you're as good as dead if you stay here. Wicker will be back before nightfall and if he doesn't kill you personally, he'll make sure that his men carry out the threat for him.'

Bret looked at the tall, beautiful woman. He was not deceived by what he saw. Under the calm exterior she was not afraid of what might happen, a true daughter of the West, but that might have been because she was in cahoots with Wicker. Bret allowed the thought to trickle through his mind, then rejected it at once.

'Why are you so all fired up about me?' he asked, walking towards the steps, keeping his eyes on the woman. He felt the grim premonition of savage violence about to break in the very near future and he knew with certainty that he would be right in the middle of it. He did not want to show his hand, but that might happen if he allowed these people to crowd him.

'It's just that I don't like to see a good man die, especially at the hands of men like these. My name is Fay Saunders. I work here. You won't get any of these people to help you, whatever it is you're trying to do. They're sheep, afraid of Wicker.'

There were angry murmurs from the crowd on the sidewalk, but she turned on them swiftly: 'Call yourselves men!' There was lashing scorn in her voice. 'One man rides into town, outdraws two of Wicker's renegades and you still stand there unable to help. When Wicker rides into town tonight, you'll run for shelter.' She turned to Bret. 'Now perhaps, you'll see what you're letting yourself in for. You're fast with a gun, probably faster than any of the gunslingers in these parts, but you can't kill them all. Sooner or later, one of them will get you.'

'I think I'll take that chance,' he said easily. 'Besides, I have a score to settle with Wicker.'

'Just who are you? State marshal? Texas Ranger?'

Bret smiled grimly, then shook his head. 'I'm not the law, far from it. But there are some things which have to be done, even outside the law.'

'if you're determined to stay in Sundown, you'll need some place to stay,' said Fay. 'And I guess my place will be as good as any.'

'But I can't put you to all of that trouble. I had thought of putting up at the saloon.'

The girl nodded. 'That's what they'd expect you to do.' She spun on a short, fat man standing on the edge of the crowd. 'Look at him. Shaking in his shoes. One word from Wicker and he'll turn you over to his gunhawks without pausing to think. I know these people. They're good men, but they're cowards.'

'I see.' Bret rubbed his chin thoughtfully. That was something he had not paused to consider. His quarrel was with Darby Wicker – no one else, and he was loathe to involve any innocent man or woman into what promised to be a gunfight, a duel to the finish. It was clear that what the girl had said was true. The townspeople of Sundown would watch with great interest and eagerness the coming events, but they would not wish to become involved too closely. Clearly Darby Wicker was a bad man to offend, a man who would remember those who turned against him for a very long time and his revenge would be swift and sure.

'I've no wish to involve you in my quarrel, ma'am,' he said quietly, turning to the girl. 'Trouble and me are never very far apart. I know Wicker of old and unless he's changed a lot since then, he'll not stop at gunning down a woman, particularly if he learns that she sheltered me.'

'Maybe I've one or two old scores to settle with him myself.' Bret saw the woman's eyes glance towards the men near at hand, eyes that were hard and speculative. A frown crossed her pretty face. As she turned to go back into the saloon she said: 'The offer is always open, stranger. If you kill Darby Wicker you'll be doing everyone in Sundown a favour, everyone that is except those card-sharps and gamblers who run these saloons.'

'I'll remember that,' he said solemnly. 'But like you say, there are too many places in this town where snakes can hide to shoot me in the back. I'll feel a mite safer out in the open.'

'Suit yourself,' said the girl with a tilt of her head. 'But don't say that I didn't warn you.' She went inside with a faint rustle of skirts and the batwing doors closed behind her.

Casually, Bret made his way into the saloon behind her, aware of the eyes on him. The bartender hastened to take up his place behind the bar. 'Think you could rustle up a couple of eggs and coffee?' asked Bret.

'Sure sure,' nodded the other hurriedly. He went through a door at the back. Bret seated himself at one of the tables, relaxing in the chair. He had the feeling that the bartender wanted him out of town before nightfall, before trouble started.

2
Night Reconnaissance

'Where are you headed for now, stranger?' asked the bartender as Bret pushed the empty plate away with a sigh of contentment and drained the coffee from the cup. 'Still think you can take on Wicker's private army single-handed? If you do, then you're a goddarned bigger fool than I took you for.'

Bret smiled. He said: 'Could be that you're right. Seems I ought to make acquaintance with Darby Wicker very soon. Do you think any of his men were in town, that they would get a message to him after I killed those men?'

The other pursed his lips. 'Could be,' he admitted. 'I don't know all of them by sight. Better ask the sheriff. He was here when all that ruckus started and he'll know if anybody does.'

'Is he in cahoots with Wicker?' Bret raised his brows slightly. 'He didn't seem ready to step in and stop their little game.'

'Wicker could have the sheriff on his pay-roll, I guess,' nodded the other slowly. 'But I don't reckon it's that way with Veldon. He's scared. He only holds his job because of Wicker's say-so. Veldon picked up one of Wicker's men on a charge of murder last night, locked him up in the jail. But he had to let him out this morning. There were too many of Wicker's men ready to swear that McKay shot in self-defence, that the two ranch hands drew first.'

'And did they?' Bret eyed him sharply, noticing every muscle of the other's face.

Slowly, the bartender shook his head. 'I was there. I saw everything that happened. Both men were shot in the back before they had a chance to go for their guns. I told that to the sheriff and those two men you killed heard me. What you saw was their way of making sure that 1 didn't talk outa turn again.'

'Then it looks as though Wicker is the man I have to do business with,' said Bret casually, pushing back his chair and rising smoothly to his feet.

'You sure are a hard-headed cuss,' said the bartender. 'But it's your funeral if you go after him.'

'That's my business, I reckon.' Bret paused at the door. 'What happened to those two gunhawks?'

The other shrugged. 'We bury them all nice and legal. It's just a pity there are so many more of them still alive.'

Bret made his way out into the street. The sun was setting now and although the heat was still there in the quiet air, the shadows were lengthening across the street and the heat devils no longer danced so viciously in the distance. A few moments later, he hit leather and headed out of Sundown, touching spurs to his mount. He now had a new choice to make. Apart from Fay Saunders, he felt he could trust no one in Sundown. Whether or not it would be possible to get the cattle ranchers together, to form them into some kind of fighting force was a matter of conjecture. There was little doubt that the man he had run into on his way into Sundown had been ready and willing to throw in his lot with him against Wicker. But at the moment, he needed someone who could handle a gun and that man had been in poor shape, would be for several weeks to come. Right now, the pressing need was for men with courage and determination and there seemed to be too few of them in the territory.

All of his thinking was bleak when he finally came upon the burnt-out ruins of the large ranch where he had found the badly injured man a few hours earlier. This was the last place that Wicker and his men would come looking for him. He did not dare risk making a fire and there was a chill in the air as he slid from the saddle, shivering a little. He did not bother to tether the horse. Between master and mount there existed an almost tangible bond born of years of comradeship, of almost perfect understanding. Ten minutes later, he rolled himself into his blankets and went to sleep, with the faint, lingering stench of wood smoke still in his nostrils.

The golden rays of the moon were shining brightly, flooding the valley with brilliance when he came suddenly awake. Swiftly. he sat up, instantly alert, his right hand going out for the gun near at hand. Close by, there came a faint snicker from the stallion, a barely audible sound in the dimness. Very carefully, he rose to his feet and edged back into the shadows of the ruins, searching the moonlight quickly with eyes and ears, every sense straining to pick out the sound which had woken him. Then he heard it again, in the distance, the drumming of hoofs, the sound of many riders spurring their mounts hard.

For a brief moment, dark dots appeared on the skyline, half a mile away. They were bunched closely together; men who did not fear watching eyes, who made no effort to hide their presence.

Something inside told him that they were Wicker's men, that possibly Wicker was riding with them and that they were up to no good, riding the range at that time of night. They were spurring their mounts over open country, scorning any of the trails in the vicinity, moving at a tangent to the spread around the ruined ranch. One glance was enough to tell Bret that they were not out looking for him in the moonlight, that they had other, more

urgent, business on hand. Reaching a sudden decision, he
whistled for the stallion, swung himself up swiftly after
throwing the rolled blankets behind the saddle.

The stallion needed no urging. Bret followed the
others' trail easily, even in the moonlight. There was no
sense in moving up too closely behind them. In the brilliant moonlight it would be possible for them to see for
close on two miles. Breasting a low rise, he found himself
staring down into a long, shallow valley, a place of rich
pasture land, in the middle of which was a cluster of buildings, a large ranch house and several barns and stables
built around it. Then realization came to him in a flash.
This was to be more of Wicker's work. Another rancher
who had obviously refused to be intimidated, or driven
away by threats, who had stubbornly refused to sell his
ranch and land for a tenth of its true value. Now, Wicker
was determined to see that he paid a far higher price than
that.

The crash of gunfire reached his ears a moment later,
as he spurred the stallion down the grassy slope. There
came the sharp, staccato answering bark of a rifle.
Whoever lived there had not been asleep, he thought
grimly; and now they were firing back. From what he had
seen of the raiders during that brief glimpse on the
skyline, there had been close on a dozen of them, as near
as he could estimate. How many there were at the ranch
capable of handling guns, it was impossible to tell. But it
was highly probable that they were heavily outnumbered.

As he drew closer to the ranch, he went more and more
cautiously. The gunhawks would not be expecting anyone
moving up from their rear, but it was best not to take
unnecessary chances. The reason he was still alive today
was because he took no chances. Dismounting behind a
small clump of hackberry trees, he went forward the rest
of the way on foot. The gunslingers had spread themselves
in a long arc in front of the ranch anti were firing inces-
santly into it. Occasionally, there came the sharp sound of

rifle fire and once he thought he heard a man scream shrilly in the dimness.

Then, quite abruptly, the firing stopped. It was very still and quiet. Bret crouched low behind a clump of bushes and strained his eyes to see in the moonlight He doubted whether all of the people defending the ranch had been killed or so incapacitated that they could no longer fire a rifle, and to think that they had run out of ammunition so soon was also unthinkable There had to be some other explanation A moment later, it was forthcoming.

As Bret crouched there in the shadows of the bushes, he saw a head rise up from the ground a little over fifty yards away, directly in front of the ranch. The man was obviously being cautious and an instant later, hearing the harsh voice, he knew why.

'All right, Redden,' shouted the man. 'This is Darby Wicker. You've had your chance. Why don't you give in and save us a lot of trouble. If we have to come in and take you, you'll regret it. This is your last warning, Redden.'

'Go to hell Wicker and take the rest of your murdering thieves with you,' yelled a voice from the darkness of the ranch house. A split second later, a rifle barked. Bret caught a fragmentary glimpse of the plume of orange flame from the muzzle and Wicker's head was hurriedly withdrawn. He heard a savage curse from the man and then a sharp order. Instantly, more guns opened up, pouring shot after shot into the building. A horse whinnied in the darkness.

Rising slowly to his feet, Bret slid away into the darkness moving quietly as a jungle cat. What little sound his feet did make, was drowned completely by the gunfire which seemed to come from all sides. As he worked his way forward, a plan of action was already forming in his mind. He recognized, at once, that in spite of the note of defiance in Redden's voice, it would be suicide for the handful of defenders to try to hold out against Wicker's band. The latter had been taking no chances when he had brought all of those men with him. It was only a matter of time before he decided to send his men around the ranch, to attack it from all sides. Once that happened, those people inside were as good as dead.

Moving with greater caution, he slithered across a patch of open ground, ducked his head as a ricocheting bullet whined over him. Pressing himself into the ground, he edged forward an inch at a time, came upon the man lying prone in the shadows before the other was aware of his presence. Before the other could turn his head, before he could yell a warning to the rest of the gunhawks, the slender blade of the knife had buried itself in his back. He sagged forward, arms thrown outward, head lolling forward in the dirt. Having satisfied himself that the man was dead, Bret removed the knife, wiped it on the other's shirt, then crawled forward again, working his way around the men who lay in a wide semicircle in front of the ranch.

Two more men died silently, without a single sound passing their lips, before he edged his way back into the shadow of the cottonwoods overlooking the ranch. Wicker's voice came clearly to him on the crisp night air. He was speaking sharply and quickly:

'All right, men, get ready to rush the house. They can't have more than a couple of men still alive. Two of you will fire the barns. The rest will burn down the house itself. I want nothing left standing. Understand?'

There were low growls of agreement. Bret tensed himself, the two guns sliding silently from their holsters. He waited until the dark figures rose up from their places of concealment saw them poised, their guns ready. Then, savagely, in unison, he opened fire. Two men swayed and fell on to their faces within as many seconds. The rest turned and tried to make out where the fire was coming from, pausing uncertainly. Dimly, Bret heard a sharp shout from the direction of the ranch. More rifles barked. Another man clutched at his chest as a bullet found its mark and stumbled against Wicker. Then the men panicked, it was what Bret had expected them to do. They would have been less than human if they had not panicked with fire cutting into them from two sides.

Wicker was desperately trying to rally them, yelling orders at the top of his bull-like voice. 'Stay where you are, you fools,' he ordered. 'There's only one of them behind us. Two of you go and get him while the rest of us take care of Redden and his men.'

For a moment, his cold, lashing voice almost succeeded in calming the men Then, sliding quickly from one concealing shadow to another, Bret opened fire again, cutting down another of the men as he tried to duck under cover. The rest of the men turned sharply and fled, firing wildly and blindly into the night as they raced for their horses. Wicker stood irresolute for a long moment, then, uttering a low curse, he turned and stumbled after them. Bret fired twice at the running, lurching figure, but missed.

The pounding of hoofs drumming away to the north was still in his ears as he made his way slowly and openly towards the ranch house. As he approached, two men came out, rifles held rock-steady in their hands. They eyed him curiously as he walked forward, then lowered their rifles when they saw that his own guns were holstered.

'Reckon we've got you to thank for driving them varmints off like that,' said one of the men. 'Lucky for us you showed up when you did. If they'd rushed us, we'd never have stood a chance.'

'I'm Sam Redden,' said the other man quietly, holding out his hand. 'I'd like to thank you properly for what you did back there. Better come into the house and clean up. Where's your mount?'

'Back there a piece.' said Bret. He whistled shrilly and a moment later, the stallion trotted up to them.

'Chet,' said Redden, turning to the other man, 'if you'll take the horse around to the stables and make him comfortable, I'll take care of our friend.'

The other nodded and Bret followed Redden into the house. They went along a short corridor and into a wide, airy room with a fire blazing brightly in the wide hearth. Redden tossed another couple of logs on to the fire, then motioned Bret to one of the chairs.

Seating himself in the other he looked at Bret from beneath lowered lids and there was a faint expression of puzzlement on his clean-cut features. He was a man in his early fifties, Bret guessed, his hair already beginning to turn grey around the temples, rather short in stature but powerfully built, his tanned, weatherbeaten skin clean-shaven. His eyes were of a deep blue and at the moment, were fastened on Bret's face with a keenness which the other found slightly disconcerting.

'Funny,' said the other, after a brief pause, 'but I seem to have the idea that we've met somewhere before. You haven't been in these parts for some time, have you?'

Bret shook his head slowly. 'Never visited Sundown or this part of the territory in my life,' he said truthfully. 'And from what I saw of Sundown today, it doesn't seem to me to be the kind of place where decent folk would want to settle. This Darby Wicker seems to have the entire place in terror of him.'

Redden gave a quick nod. 'If he once discovers that you killed those men out there, he won't rest until you're dead.'

A grim smile played momentarily over Bret's lips. 'There are two more dead men in Sundown to testify against me.

Redden raised his brows. 'Two of Wicker's men?'

'That's right. They were shooting up one of the bartenders in the Golden Ace saloon. Guess he said the wrong thing in their hearing They had their guns in their hands when I called 'em.'

'You got something against Wicker?' Redden looked at him closely, almost as if daring him to deny it.

'I've an old score to settle with him,' admitted Bret,

'Perhaps I should introduce myself. The name's Bret Manders. I've been looking for Darby Wicker for close on seven years. It wasn't until six months ago, down in Alabama, that I heard he had headed this way when the war finished. I finally tracked him down yesterday. Seems I came just in time. There must be a lot of men who'd dearly love to kill him.'

'You ain't too late, that's for certain,' said the other quietly. He rose to his feet, walked across to the corner of the room and poured two drinks, handing one to Bret. 'And we're mighty glad to have you around, believe me. There are few men in the territory who dare stand up to Wicker and his army of killers. We need every man we can get if we're to stop him and his gang from ruining everything we've tried to build up here around Sundown. It would be a decent frontier town if we could only get rid of him and his pack of coyotes.'

'I gather that the sheriff can't be depended upon to help.' Bret sipped his drink slowly. The raw spirit stung the back of his throat, then slid down into his stomach where it exploded in a hazy cloud of warmth.

'He's yeller,' growled the other, lowering himself into the chair. He looked at Bret appraisingly. 'But you look to me to be a man who's handy with a gun and now that you've already killed several of Wicker's men, you're in this deal up to the neck with the rest of us. You weren't thinking of staying in Sundown, were you?'

Bret shook his head. 'I figgered that wouldn't be a very wise thing to do with so many of Wicker's men in town. I intended spending the rest of the night in that ranch they burned yesterday. I was there when I heard their party heading in this direction and figgered I'd better take a look-see.'

'Glad you did,' said the other gratefully. 'But you'll stay here with me and I'll not take no for an answer. After what you did tonight, you're entitled to everything I can do to help you. I'm in your debt, Bret, and, as anyone will tell you, I'm a man who always pays his debts in full.'

Bret stretched his legs thankfully towards the warm fire.
'I'm only too glad to accept your offer,' he said wearily.
'Tell me, what do you know about a girl called Fay
Saunders?'

'Fay Saunders?' There was a note of surprise in the
other's voice. 'She's a singer in the Golden Ace saloon.
Why should you be interested in her?'

'She made the same offer as you've just done. I gathered that she was no friend of Wicker's either. If that's
true, she could be of great help to us.'

'I'm afraid I don't quite see that.'

'We need someone we can trust in Sundown. You and I
would probably be shot on sight by any of Wicker's men.
But she might be able to get information for us. If we knew
his plans in advance, we could make some of our own.'

'That's a good thing,' nodded Redden. Glancing up as
the other man came into the room, he said: 'Chet here
will get you a bite to eat. In the meantime, I'll try to put
you wise to what's been happening around here.'

When the other had gone out of the room, Redden
filled his pipe and lit it until it was drawing to his satisfaction. 'I guess everything started about a couple of years
back. Sundown was just a small place then, a regular frontier town. Sheriff Masson kept law and order but the only
trouble we had in those days came when a few of the boys
got a little liquored up and started shooting off their guns
in town. Then, the homesteaders started coming in from
the East. All in all, they were welcome here. We gave them
land and they brought a measure of prosperity to
Sundown. Stores and saloons set up business. Then, Darby
Wicker arrived in Sundown. Nobody knew much about
him except that he had been a landowner back East and
had come West to seek new opportunities. He bought the
old Weston ranch south of Sundown when the old man
died and started to build up a herd of cattle there. It's a
big ranch, well pastured and well watered. Pretty soon, he
had a herd of several thousand head.

'But after a while, it soon became obvious that he wasn't content even with that. There was some rustling started but we couldn't pin it down to anyone in particular, least of all Wicker. He was a clever man and whenever anyone protested, he gave them permission to examine the brands on his cattle – the Lazy V – and they never found anything out of order there. But when he brought in some gunslingers from way back East, things soon came to a showdown. It was over at Carson's spread that it started. He'd been losing a few head of cattle on and off for the best part of a year and when he caught the rustlers red-handed he gave his boys the order to start shooting first and ask questions later. The upshot of it all was that they killed a couple of men and later identified them as men who worked for Wicker.'

He paused as Chet came back and laid a plate of roast lamb and potatoes in front of Bret, then went on slowly: 'Carson upped and went to Sheriff Masson, taking the bodies with him. This was the first time that anyone could prove that Wicker's men were responsible for what was happening in the territory.'

'Go on,' said Bret, as the other paused. 'What happened then?' He chewed reflectively on the food. It was the first time he had eaten anything like this and he realized just how hungry he really was. Bacon and beans on the trail had dulled his appreciation of the finer things.

'Sheriff Masson got a posse together and rode over to the Lazy V ranch to have it out with Wicker. Seems that he was tipped off however, because they were ambushed in Drygulch Canyon. Masson was shot in the back and half of the posse were killed. After that, Wicker really moved in and took over Sundown. He put Veldon into the sheriff's office, knowing that he had him under his thumb, could make him do exactly as he wanted. Anyone who says anything against him is either shot or thrown into jail by Veldon. Any of his own men who're arrested on any charge, are set free the next day. Don't get the idea that

Veldon is in Wicker's pay. He isn't. He hates Wicker as much as the rest of us, but he's scared for his own skin. He won't do anything to risk that.'

'And the other ranchers around Sundown. What about them? Why don't they just band together and ride against Wicker? Surely if they did that they would outnumber him by three to one. Wouldn't that be the simplest way of getting rid of Wicker'?'

'Believe me, Bret,' said the other earnestly. 'That's what I've been aiming for ever since this started. But it isn't as easy as you think. They're scared too. Wicker tries to buy them out, offering them about half of what their spread is worth. If they refuse, and most of them do, he attacks their ranches, kills or rustles their cattle, burns their crops and ranch houses. He's picking us all off one by one and they're too stupid to see it. United, we would stand a chance. But as it is, he'll drive every one of us out within the year unless a miracle happens.'

Bret smiled thinly. 'in my experience, miracles don't just happen. You have to make them come about.' He pushed the empty plate away and leaned back in his chair. 'And what about the military. Aren't there troops over at Fort Laramie? Ever thought of asking them for help?'

'Sure. But that isn't so easy, I'm afraid. We've sent through for help, but it seems we have an enlightened government who believe that, with the Indians subdued, with the War over, there's no need to keep a lot of troops to defend the frontier. The bad old days are over as far as Washington are concerned and men like Wicker are stepping in and taking advantage of this. The commander at Fort Laramie can't spare even a company of men to come down here and take over control of Sundown until all of this is sorted out.'

'I see.' Bret nodded slowly 'Things are worse than I had thought. The cards are all stacked on Wicker's side. If we're to do anything at all, we'll have to act fast. If we waste any time, he'll he in an impregnable position.'

'What do you suggest that we do?' There was a weary despair in the other's deep voice. We've tried just about everything we can think of.'

'Except fighting back.' There was a lashing bite to Bret's voice as he leaned forward in his chair. 'That's the only way you'll get rid of this snake. If you sit back and accept it's inevitable that he'll run you out of the territory, then he'll do it.'

Redden spread his hands defensively. 'How can we fight back, Bret? He has a private army of close on fifty hired gunmen, all of them professional killers that he pays well just to make sure there is no trouble. And if things do show any sign of getting out of hand, then he can send south of the border into Mexico and bring up more roughnecks to swell his ranks.'

'There's one powerful force here which only needs prodding into action for it to overthrow Wicker and every-thing he stands for,' declared Bret with conviction.

'There is?' Redden glanced up at him in mild surprise.

'The homesteaders and the decent townsfolk of Sundown. If we can only show them that there's some way of defeating Wicker, I think they'll rally round.'

'I only wish you were right.' The other's face lost its momentary look of hope. 'But I'm afraid you won't be able to count upon them to help us. They know Wicker of old. Like Sheriff Veldon, they're too concerned with their own precious hides to care what happens to us and they're too short-sighted to see that once he's taken over the cattle ranches, he'll start on them.'

Bret rolled himself a cigarette and lit it with an ember from the fire. 'So we have to start with what we have at the moment. Well, at least, we gave them a licking tonight which they won't forget in a hurry.'

'Thanks to your intervention,' nodded the other. 'I'll place guards around the spread tonight although I doubt whether they'll be back. Wicker will want to gather together more of his men before he tries agin. But he'll be back, you can be sure of that. He won't be able to take a defeat like this lying down.'

'Nonetheless, we've got to hit him again, before he expects it and hit him hard. If we can get him rattled, lie might make a fatal mistake. 'That's when we'll have him.'

'My God, Bret, but you've given me new hope,' declared the other, getting to his feet. 'Just when I figgered that all hope was gone. I'd like you to talk to the rest of the ranchers in these parts like you've talked to me. You might swing them all around to your way of thinking.'

'It's worth a try.' Bret rose slowly and stood beside the table. He knew, deep down inside, that he faced a very dangerous mission, far more tricky and dangerous than any he had known before. But he faced the prospect with a cool and calm confidence which came of long experience and he quiet courage which was a characteristic part of his nature.

'I'll have you a bed made up,' said the other as he walked towards the door. 'You must have ridden quite a few miles in the past few days. Don't worry about another attack. The boys will keep a sharp look out for any of that bunch who might try to make a sneak attack.'

As Redden had prophesied, the night passed without incident. Evidently, Wicker had given up the idea of attacking the ranch for the time being.

When Bret made the rounds of the perimeter wire with a couple of the boys, he found that the bodies of the men who had been killed during the night had been taken away. At breakfast, he mentioned this to Redden, who nodded slowly:

'Very likely they decided to send a couple of their men back for them,' he said, quite unconcernedly. 'We certainly didn't bury the coyotes.'

'You mean that they managed to get so close without being seen by your guards'?' Bret looked at him in astonishment.

The other shook his head, smiling. 'They were seen all

right, but my men didn't fire on them. It was quite unnecessary. There were just two of them.'

'I'm glad you take it all so casually,' Bret grinned. 'I
think I'll take a ride into Sundown this morning. There
are one or two questions I'd like to ask of the sheriff and I
think I can persuade him to give me the right answers.'

'Be careful, Bret,' warned the other seriously. 'The Lazy
V *hombres* may be there already and they'll be on the look
out for you.'

'Maybe. I'm not sure though. The only two men who
have seen me face to face – Wicker's men, I mean – are
dead. It may be that there were others in the crowd, biding
their time, but that's a chance I'll have to take. I want to
know what Wicker is doing and, more important still, what
he intends to do.'

'And you figger that Sheriff Veldon will tell you?'

'Could be. If he doesn't, then I know somebody who
will.'

'Fay Saunders?'

'That's right. I hate dragging her into this. If Wicker
should ever find out, he could make it hard for her. But
there's a lot at stake here, far more than I thought when I
first arrived. I figgered I had only to even my score with
Wicker and that was it finished as far as I was concerned. I
see now that I was wrong. There's a lot more people
involved.'

'Mebbe you're right to go, but go careful. They're a
murdering bunch of hoodlums and they'll shoot you in
the back if they ever get the chance. I don't want to pry
into your own business, Bret. I've got troubles enough of
my own. But it figgers that if you've a score to settle with
Wicker, there's been bad blood between the two of you at
some time in the past and he'll recognize you.'

'Don't worry about me, old-timer,' Bret nodded grimly.
'I've had plenty of experience in looking after my own
hide. I don't aim to do anything foolish in Sundown.'

'I'll have Chet saddle your mount,' promised the other.

Half an hour later, Bret rode away from the Redden ranch and headed towards Sundown.

Passing through the boundary wire, Bret allowed the stallion to pick its own pace and sat easily in the saddle, keen eyes surveying the surrounding territory. Far in the distance to his left, where the hills rose in a shading of purple haze, he could just make out a large herd of cattle on the nearer slopes. From the directions which Redden had given him the previous night, he guessed that this was the Lazy V spread, Wicker's ranch.

Now that the sun had risen the day was good and warm but with no sense of oppression in its heat as there had been on the previous day. The sky was wide and cloudless over his head, reaching down out of the endless infinities to touch the purple hills which lay across the northern horizon. He had chosen this route into Sundown deliberately, riding high over the surrounding countryside so that he might keep an eye on the lowland trail, where any of Wicker's men might be expecting him. From here, he could look down into the valley and see in both directions for several miles. He figured that if anyone was trailing him the sooner he knew about it, the better. But even though he glanced over his shoulder several times, he saw no one and the valley trail stretched away into the distance, completely deserted.

Then, shortly before noon, glancing back, he saw the small cloud of dust in the distance and reined his mount in the shadow of a clump of tall trees. The riders, whoever they were, were coming up fast, spurring their mounts to the utmost. As they came nearer, he saw that there were three of them, men who were in a hurry, men who rode with a purpose.

If they were tailing him, he decided, if they had been watching the Redden ranch, waiting for someone to ride out, then they would soon be very puzzled men and it would take them some time to realize that he had been a mite too clever for them and had taken the higher trail. By the time the realization hit them, he would have circled around and entered Sundown from the west. He smiled grimly to himself. No matter what these men did, he would be in the town before them and would have the chance to get everything he needed out of the sheriff.

A mile further on, the trail dipped through a narrow valley, between rising clefts of sandstone and rock. Before he urged the stallion down into it, out of it of the valley trail, he threw a swiftly appraising glance behind him. The three riders were now almost level with him on the valley trail and they were riding very slowly now, trying to pick up his trail. He pulled the brim of his hat down over his eyes with a characteristic gesture. It would not take them too long to figure out what had happened, he told himself and then they would either head straight for town to try head him off or light out over the country to spread the news to Wicker He could guess what the other's reactions would be when he heard how his men had. bungled even this mission.

As he rode on, circling the lower trail, he found the calm silence a balm, giving him a much-needed chance to think things out, to examine them objectively. Whatever happened, it was essential that he should plan ahead. He had to keep one jump ahead of Wicker if he wanted to stay alive, and if these ranchers were to rid the place of these crooks and killers.

He rode in over the bridge and entered the main street of Sundown, eyes alert beneath the wide-brimmed hat. There were several people on the streets and a crowd of men in front of the Golden Ace saloon. But none of them paid him any attention as he rode slowly forward, stopping in front of the sheriff's office and strode inside.

Veldon was seated at the low table on the far side of the room when he entered and looked up swiftly. For a moment, his face was blank, devoid of all expression. Then a look of swift recognition appeared in his eyes and he thrust back his chair so quickly that it almost fell over behind him. He got to his feet and stood looking at Bret like a frightened rabbit.

'What are you doing back in town?' he asked, finally finding his voice. 'I thought I warned you to get out of Sundown and head for open country yesterday.'

'Why now, Sheriff, I guess you did,' said Bret casually. He indicated the other to sit down again. For a moment, the sheriff looked as if he intended to resist, then he flopped down into the chair, mopping at his fleshy face with a large red handkerchief. Sweat had popped out on his forehead and was running in little rivulets down his face, into his eyes.

'I guess you know that Wicker is mad about those two men of his you killed yesterday. He's already sworn out a warrant for your arrest.'

'On what charge?' asked Bret mildly, smiling faintly.

'Murder,' said the other, jerking the word out almost defiantly. 'He claims you shot them both in the back without giving them a chance to draw.'

Bret nodded, unsurprised. 'I figgered he would do something like that,' he said conversationally. 'That's what he always does, isn't it? Manipulates the law as he sees fit. And how do you propose to execute that warrant, Sheriff? I'm here, why not try to arrest me?'

He smiled at the expression on the other's face. Veldon licked his lips nervously, slumping into his chair. 'Well, now,' he began, 'even though he does have several witnesses who are—'

'I know, they're all ready to swear that they saw me shoot them down in the back. Unfortunately, right now, I've got a lot more on my mind than to worry about Wicker and his warrants. You know as well as I do that it was a fair fight. They had their guns in their hands before I drew. But I didn't come here to talk about that.'

He imagined that he saw a look of relief spread itself momentarily over the other's fat face, but he couldn't be sure because it was gone almost before it had appeared. 'I suppose that you know there was another attack last night. On the Redden ranch. They tried to drive off his cattle and fire his ranch house and barns.'

'I did hear something about it, but no details,' said the other hesitantly. 'But how come you know so much about it?'

'I was there,' said Bret calmly. 'I killed three of his men and I'd have killed Wicker only he ran so fast when he realized that things were going against him. But there's no doubt in my mind that he'll try again, if not at the Redden ranch, then somewhere else. I want to know where he's going to strike next.'

'And you want me to give you that information?' asked the other incredulously. 'You must be crazy.' He got unsteadily to his feet. 'Mister, I don't know who you are, or why you came here. But let me give you a word of advice. Don't try to fight Darby Wicker. You don't stand a chance of success.'

'Could be that you're right. On the other hand, you might be wrong. It seems to me that he's been having too much of his own way around these parts in the past two years. It's time somebody put a stop to it.'

The other glanced about him furtively, as if expecting to be overheard. 'If I do tell you, there'll be no way of Wicker getting to know who gave you the information? You promise me that.'

'I promise.' Bret knew now that he had not underestimated the fat sheriff. He could see exactly how the other's mind was working. The chances of Wicker being defeated were extremely remote; but in the event that a miracle did occur, then Veldon wanted to be sure that he was on the winning side.

'I heard about last night from one of the men. Wicker isn't feeling too happy after that defeat. It's the first he's ever had in these parts and he knows what it means. If he shows that he can't handle the situation, then the townspeople are going to come down off the fence and side against him. When that happens, his number's up.'

'Exactly.' Bret gave a quick nod. Time was running out swiftly. Those three riders must be nearing Sundown now unless they had ridden straight to Wicker. 'But I still want to know where he intends to strike next.'

'I'm not sure. I did hear them mention that Clem Nolan had refused to accept Wicker's offer, that this time there was going to be no mistake.'

'Clem Nolan,' Bret nodded. At the moment, he had no idea where that particular spread might be, but Redden would know. He moved slowly towards the door. 'I wouldn't mention our little conversation to anyone, Veldon,' he said warningly. 'Particularly to Wicker. If you do, you can take it from me that I'll come hunting you down and you'll find that my vengeance is as quick and as sure as his.' He wasn't sure how far he could trust this man. A coward was one of the men it was difficult to trust. If Wicker suspected that he had been to see Veldon, he would apply the pressure on the sheriff and there was little doubt that the other would talk.

I'm leaving now,' he said quietly. 'Don't try to follow me if you value your life. I've little time for men who are supposed to uphold the law, but who make a mockery of it because of a coyote like Wicker.'

Opening the door, he stepped out on to the boardwalk, climbed swiftly into the saddle and rode swiftly along the dusty street. He was aware of eyes boring into his back and knew that the sheriff was watching his departure closely. Reaching the end of the street, instead of heading back across the country, he wheeled his mount, cut in behind the houses which bordered the street. Ten minutes later, he reached the back of the Golden Ace saloon and swung out of the saddle. If any of Wicker's men decided to trail him out of town, they were in for a disappointment.

He reached for the handle of the door, twisted it sharply and found, as he had anticipated, that it was not locked. Swiftly, he stepped inside, closing the door softly behind him. He found himself in a long hallway with a row of pegs on the wall. There were three gun belts hanging on them, each with two Colt .45s in them. So whoever ran this gambling saloon made the men shuck their guns, he reflected. At least, that helped him. There was no one in sight as he moved, cat-footed, along the corridor, reached a corner and peered around it. In spite of the fact that he had saved the bartender's life two days earlier, he doubted whether the other would have enough guts to help him in the face of Wicker's vengeance. There was only Fay Saunders who had come to his help openly in front of the rest of the townsfolk and any of the Lazy V hands who might have been in the crowd.

In front of him, a flight of narrow stairs led to the upper floor and he made his way cautiously up them, reaching the wide landing at the top. Here, there was another long passage with doors leading off either side. Even as he stood there, irresolute, one of the doors opened. His gun was in his hand before it was fully open and a tall, slender figure stood framed in the doorway.

'Well, if it isn't my sharp-shooter friend,' said a warm, husky voice. 'Don't tell me that you're going to shoot me now?'

He lowered the gun. 'Not exactly, Fay,' he said quietly, 'but even here, you are never sure of what kind of welcome you might get.'

'The very fact that you're still around means that you must be looking for trouble.' She motioned him inside the room, closing the door behind him. 'Did anyone see you come here?'

He shook his head. 'I visited the sheriff a little while ago, then rode out of town a little way before heading back.'

'Was it wise to see Veldon?' She arched her delicately pencilled eyebrows. 'He's in cahoots with Wicker, you know.'

'That's why I went to see him. I want to know where Wicker intends to strike next. There's just the chance that I can get enough men from the other ranches together to make things hot for him and his men.'

'You're asking for big trouble.' She lowered herself into the chair in front of the large mirror.. 'He's a dangerous man. Nobody knows much about him. Perhaps that's part of his strength.'

'Or his weakness,' said Bret thinly. 'You see, I happen to know everything about him. I know what he was during the war, how he got his wealth, and that he's wanted by both the law and the Army authorities.'

She nodded. 'Somehow, I thought there had to be something like that between the two of you. Were you in the war together?'

'We both fought for the South, if that's what you mean.' Bret was deliberately guarded. It was still possible that Fay Saunders was playing a double game, that this conversation would get back to Wicker, word for word.

'I see.' She was silent for several moments, powdering her face with slow, delicate movements. 'Then it can't be a case of different ideals. So there has to be something else.'

'I wouldn't let that worry you none.' Bret could feel her eyes on him again, appraising him, trying to figure him out. 'That episode has nothing to do with anyone but Darby Wicker and me. Because of it, one of us is going to die now that I've finally run him to earth. This is nothing to do with what's been happening here since he came into town.'

She shrugged her shoulders. 'I'm not worrying,' she said coolly. 'If you want to kill Wicker, that's your business. But you aren't going to find it easy. There are at least fifty men that he can call on at a moment's notice and more over the Mexican border who'll come running once he sends the word.'

'So I gather. I aim to stop him sending the word.'

'You're talking mighty big for one man aren't you.' He

wasn't sure whether it was disdain or an admiring curiosity in her voice as she turned in her chair to stare at him. 'Just how do you propose to do that?'

'That's my affair. All I want at the moment is someone inside Sundown to check on his movements, on what his men are doing. So far, you're the only one here I feel I can trust.'

She smiled. 'Why, thank you.' Then she was instantly serious. 'I like you. Whether or not you're on the right side of the law, I don't care. All I do know is that Darby Wicker has been killing and rustling long enough. Sooner or later, Sundown will cease to be a frontier town It's going to grow and it'll become a decent, safe place to live in. But not while there are men like that around. He's got to be stopped before he can go any further and if you're the man who can stop him, then I'll help you. What do you want me to do?'

'Do you think it will be possible for you to slip out of town every couple of days without arousing any suspicion?'

'I think so. I often go for a drive in the country. Once or twice, Wicker has come with me, but he won't pay any attention if I go alone.'

'Good. I want you to keep a sharp watch on what happens in town. I've a feeling that the sheriff will try to get in touch with Wicker, tell him that I've been here asking awkward questions. You can also try your hand at getting some information from the Lazy V hands who come into the saloon. When they're drunk, they'll tell you anything you want to know. That information can be useful to us.'

'Us?' She looked at him closely, a look of curiosity in her eyes.

'That's right,' he answered easily. 'I've an idea that pretty soon, more and more of the ranchers, and perhaps the homesteaders are going to settle their differences and throw in their lot with Redden and myself. They must see that it's the only possible way there is to defeat Wicker.'

'I'll get what you want.'

'I knew you would,' he said warmly. 'Meet me tomorrow at noon where the river cuts across the Redden spread. Can you find the place?'

'I'll be there.' She rose swiftly to her feet at the sound of raucous laughter from down below. 'Now you'd better get out of here and put some distance between yourself and Sundown. Sounds as though the customers are starting to arrive.'

'Take care of yourself,' he said quietly, as he opened the door and threw a swift look along the corridor. 'Above all, don't do anything that might make Wicker or any of his men suspicious. I don't want to lose my only source of information in Sundown.'

He walked swiftly along the corridor, down the narrow stairs and out through the rear entrance. A man's voice was shouting something gruffly in the bar as he went out. Seconds later, he was in the saddle, hitting leather as he rode out of Sundown. Behind him, the town drowsed in the noon heat and ahead of him, the desert trail stretched eastwards towards the Redden ranch,

He wondered if Wicker had any inkling that there was a plan being built up against him in Sundown, that there was unrest in the empire which he had built here, based on fear and terror. If he did, what would he do about it? Call in the Mexican half-breeds from across the border – or muster his own killers, hand-picked men whom he could trust implicitly? There was danger for everyone concerned whichever he did.

3

Gunsmoke Over Sundown

Bret Manders and Sam Redden rode slowly, side by side, along the trail which skirted the river just inside the boundary of the spread. It still wanted another twenty minutes to noon, but from their vantage point, they could see for almost two miles along the trail which led into Sundown.

'You think she'll come, Bret?' asked Redden after a short pause. He reined his mount, shading his eyes against the sunlight and staring along the trail. 'I'm not sure that you were wise to trust her. What's to stop her bringing half of Wicker's men behind her?'

'Nothing, I guess. But somehow, I reckon she's the one straight person in Sundown. I don't know why she hates Wicker so much, but I'm sure that she does.'

'All right, Bret. I'll go along with you. As you say, we need this information if we're to stand any chance of beating Wicker at his own game. But even assuming that she does confirm he intends to attack Clem Nolan's place and can give us the time, how can we expect to fight off the number of men he can send? He won't take any chances at all this time, you know. There'll be close on fifty men with him when he rides against the Nolan spread.'

'That's what I figger too,' agreed the other as he slid from the saddle. 'And we too, will have a little surprise ready for them.'

Ten minutes later, there was a cloud of dust in the distance, along the Sundown trail and as they waited, the shape of a small carriage, drawn by two high-stepping horses materialized out of the dust and headed in their direction.

'Doesn't look as though she's brought anyone with her,' said Bret. He slid the Colt .45 back into its holster. 'Let's hope she has some news for us.'

Fay Saunders could evidently handle the horses well and Bret watched with admiration as she reined them to a halt. He went forward and helped her down.

She threw Redden a quick glance, then smiled at Bret. 'Somehow, I don't think your friend likes me,' she said with a charming frankness.

'That isn't really true,' he said quickly. 'But at the moment, he trusts no one, I'm afraid. There are too many people in the pay of Darby Wicker for him to take any chances.'

'I think I understand.' She adjusted the long white gloves. She said gravely: 'There were a lot of Lazy V boys in town yesterday and more this morning. They were obviously getting ready to ride soon.'

'Did you find out when – and where?' he asked.

She nodded. 'You were right about this man, Nolan. Wicker is hopping mad after the way he and his men were treated when they came here. He's determined that this time nobody is going to stand in his way. I reckon he intends to take out the whole of his killer outfit. They're ready to ride tonight.'

'I see. At least that confirms what the sheriff told me. Did you find out anything else?'

'Only that there were a couple of Wicker's men in the

crowd that day you shot up those two men in Sundown. They must have described you to him because it seems he knows who you are.'

'What makes you so sure about that?' asked Bret sharply.

'Wicker was in the saloon last night with his ranch foreman and six of his men. I was singing as usual and I managed to work my way over to their table. I overheard him say that it was imperative they got rid of someone who could make real trouble for him if he wasn't silenced right away. Someone called Bret Manders. I figured that might be you.'

Bret chuckled thinly. 'So he's finally wise to me,' he said easily. 'Well, I suppose it had to come some time. He'll be on his guard now, I guess.'

'You seem to be enjoying the prospect of what's coming,' she said archly. 'You must hate Wicker to want to kill him so badly – and the same goes for him. I got the idea he was more scared of you than all the other ranchers in the territory put together.'

'Mebbe he has a real cause to be scared.' Bret tightened his lips into a thin line across his handsome features. 'As far as the ranchers are concerned, he's merely trying to take their homesteads, their cattle and ranches away from them. He took far more than that away from me – and he knows he'll have to answer for it. That's why he's so afraid.'

There was something intense and harsh in his voice as he spoke and his eyes seemed fixed on something in the far distance, something which neither of the other two could see. After a brief moment, he seemed to stir himself, gave a brief nod and said in his usual, bantering tone: 'But first we have to make sure that he doesn't carry out his threat of burning the Nolan ranch to the ground tonight.'

'I wish I could see how you intend to do that,' growled Redden. 'I can let you have six men, men that I can trust and who're handy with a gun. I can also get word across to Nolan this afternoon, warn him of the trouble that's coming. But all that isn't going to stop fifty hardened killers.'

'Perhaps not. But I noticed something at your place yesterday which will help us.' Bret dug in the pocket of his shirt and pulled out a slender yellow stick which he tossed from hand to hand, Redden's eyes widened at what he saw.

'Dynamite,' he muttered softly. 'There's plenty of that. I got it in some time ago when there was talk of opening the old silver mine at the north-eastern corner of my spread. But it was never used. I see your plan all right now, but the problem is how are you going to do it?'

'We'll work that out this afternoon. Thanks to Fay here, we're forewarned and we still have several hours before those gunhawks start to ride.' He turned to the girl. 'In the meantime, I reckon you'd better get back into Sundown, Fay, in case anyone misses you. We don't want Wicker to suspect that we know anything of his plans.'

They waited until the carriage had faded into the distance before turning and making their way back to the ranch.

During the whole of that afternoon, while they had worked, aided by six men from Reddon's ranch, Bret had felt the tension beginning to mount. It was not easy work, but Sam Redden had been true to his promise, had warned Clem Nolan of what Wicker intended to do, and most of the time they had worked along the narrow, rocky trail which led south towards Nolan's ranch, the trail along which the Lazy V hands would have to ride when they attacked that night.

The sticks of dynamite had been carefully laid at strategic positions along the trail, most of it among the rocks which overhung the narrow track at places where the rocky walls rose sheer for almost twenty feet on either side. Long powder trails had been run from the dynamite to a point where it would be easy to ignite several trains at once. There would be little warning of the approach of the enemy and there could be no mistake when handling anything as tricky and as dangerous as this. The man who lit the powder trains had to have a chance of getting away before the charges detonated.

By nightfall, everything was ready. The moon came up, round and full less than half an hour after sunset and there was no darkness to speak of. By ten o'clock, everyone was in position. Bret himself was to light the first train of powder fuses and he had chosen a vantage point overlooking the trail where he was able to see for several hundred yards in either direction. Whatever happened, he had also to be sure that all of his men too, were under cover before he fired the trains of gunpowder.

As he crouched there in the thick brush which dotted the rocky ground, he listened to the strange quietness of the night, a quietness that was not quite silence, but something compounded of the tiny, half-heard sounds of the night. In the distance, a coyote howled mournfully, in a dismal wail to the full moon.

For some strange reason, the sound sent a little shiver along his spine and he found himself clutching the box of sulphur matches a little more tightly than was really necessary. A little while later, as the moon rose higher into the clear, cloudless sky, a little breeze sprang up, a cold breeze that made him shiver slightly as he lay there, eyes staring into the flooding moonlight, ears trying to pick out the faintest sound in the distance. By now, if they really intended to carry out their threat, Wicker and his men would have left Sundown, would be on their way to fire the Nolan ranch. He smiled grimly to himself in the dimness, wondering whether Wicker had even guessed that something might happen to spoil his plans. With fifty picked and hardened killers at his back, he would fondly imagine himself to be secure, would never believe that anyone would be foolish enough to try anything against a band that size.

But this time, if everything went accordingly, he would

find himself outsmarted once again, although Bret
doubted if it would be the knockout blow as far as Wicker
was concerned. Even with the dynamite, they could not
hope to kill off all of these men. There would still be
plenty of them remaining alive to fight another day. He
eased his body into a more comfortable position. Sharp
stabbing pains of cramp were shooting through his legs.
Not long to wait now, he told himself. So long as the handful of men with him did not panic. If they stood their
ground and concentrated their fire, they stood an excellent chance of breaking Wicker's men, of throwing them
back long before they got within striking distance of the
ranch itself.

He rolled himself a cigarette and carefully shielded the
flame with his hands, acutely conscious of the powder spread
over the ground a few feet away. It needed only one spark to
set those gunpowder trains on fire, to send the flame hissing
and pluttering towards the sticks of carefully concealed
dynamite. Whatever happened, the explosive had not to go
off prematurely. That would give the killers sufficient warning, a chance to get under cover and use their tremendous
advantage in numbers to overwhelm them.

He threw a swift glance into the moonlit darkness
behind him, but there was no sign of the men who
crouched in wait, ready to use their guns whenever he
gave the order. But the very knowledge that they were
there, made him feel a little better. If everything went well
this night, it would go a long way towards forcing the
townsfolk, the other ranchers and the homesteaders, to
join them, to take up arms against Wicker and drive him
out of the territory before he could bring in any more
killers from across the border.

For an hour, there was not a single sound, except for
the rustle of some nocturnal animal in the brush and the
distant wail of a coyote. Then, Bret heard it, far-away but
coming closer, the drumming of hoofs on the hard
ground. The Lazy V riders were on their way and he felt

the muscles of his stomach tense themselves into hard knots as he lay and waited for them to get sufficiently close for him to light the fuses.

Now he could hear the rest of the men moving around restlessly in the brush and he called out for them to stay under cover, repeating his warning that they were not to open fire until he gave the word. Once the dynamite exploded, and confusion among the enemy was complete, it would be concentrated volleys of accurate fire that would be needed.

'Here they come now,' Redden's voice reached him from the darkness and turning his head, he saw the small knot of black dots in the moon-washed distance, where the trail wound upwards into the rocks. They were closely bunched together, riding swiftly and with a singleness of purpose that sent a little apprehensive shiver though Bret's body. What chance did his little band have against so many men, if anything went wrong with the dynamite? It was something he did not want to think about, not at that particular moment, and he swiftly pushed the thought out of his mind as he pulled the box of sulphur matches from his pocket and held them ready, aware of the quiet thudding of his heart against his ribs.

The riders swept on into the rocky defile. If they were suspecting an ambush, surely this would be the place for it, but they never once hesitated. It was as if they were supremely confident that they were riding in sufficient numbers to brush aside any opposition they might encounter. Bret felt his lips twitch into a grimace of derision. If they only knew what they were riding into, he thought grimly.

He waited for another minute, then struck the match and applied it swiftly to the very centre of the powder trains. Within seconds, red flame was dancing swiftly among the rocks, completely invisible to anyone down below. Scrambling to his feet as silently as possible, he moved further back into the rocks to join the others.

'Is it lit?' queried Sam Nolan in a hoarse, throaty whisper.

Bret nodded. 'Another few moments and they'll start to go off,' he promised. 'And when they do, they'll bring half of that rock tumbling down about those killers' heads.'

He held his head low. Even here, some thirty yards or so from the nearest point of explosion, there was still a definite danger from falling rock. Very carefully, he eased the Colts from their holsters, held them balanced in his hands. The first explosion came a few seconds later, shattering the quiet of the night, hammering at their eardrums. Close on the heels of the detonations, came the dull rumble of tons of rock sliding down on to the narrow trail. Both sides had been mined with dynamite and lifting his head cautiously, Bret was able to see a minor avalanche pouring down on top of the leading group of men as they rode forward, their mounts screaming shrilly as the rock crashed around them, crushing them before they could break free.

'Rapid fire.' Bret raised his voice so that the men on the far side of the trail could hear him too. The dull echoes of the falling rock had barely died away before the crashing volley of gunfire hammered out. Men and horses struggled desperately to get free of the thunderous explosions, only to be met by a hail of bullets which plucked them from their saddles and pitched them dead on to the trail. Instantly, there was confusion among the men on the trail. Bret could hear them yelling to each other as they tried to get under cover. They had no way of telling whether any more dynamite might go off and the thought must have added to their fear.

Rising to his feet, shooting from the hip as he went forward, Bret strode to the rocky ledge overlooking the trail some twenty feet below him, a trail which was in shadow, where the moonlight did not penetrate. Down there, men were reining their horses and trying to get out of the saddle before the terrified beasts carried them out

into the open where they would be picked off with ease by
the men crouched among the rocks on either side of the
trail.

Swiftly, Bret climbed to the top of the rock ledge. The
dynamite had done its work well, trapping more than a
dozen men and their mounts beneath the rocks which had
come raining down on them from both sides. But he saw
that the majority of the Lazy V riders, moving up behind
the leading force when the charges detonated, had been
sufficiently clear of the explosion to escape most of the
blast and were already scattering for cover. In the moonlight, it was difficult to estimate how many of them there
were, or even if Darby Wicker had decided to ride with
them again.

Instinctively, Bret pulled down his head as a shot ricocheted off the rocks near at hand, cursing himself savagely
as he realized that he had committed the cardinal sin of
showing himself clearly against the skyline. That shot had
been too close for comfort and it indicated that the Lazy
V hands, far from being routed and confused by what had
happened, were already beginning to take the initiative
from him.

Redden came crawling forward out of the darkness and
crouched down beside him: 'You all right, Bret?' There
was a note of concern in his deep voice.

'Sure, I'm all right.' Bret fired instinctively at two shadows that came lurching out of the smoke and dust on the
far side of the trail. One of the gunhawks uttered a low
cough and fell back. His companion snapped a quick shot
in their direction, aiming wild, then bent and dragged the
other man under cover.

'Thought you'd been hit bad by the way you went
down,' went on Redden, apparently unconcerned. 'What
do we do now? Hold them here or pull back to the ranch.
It ain't going to be long before they figger out just how
many men we have here and then they'll leave a dozen or
so to keep us pinned down, while the rest work their way

around us and head straight for Nolan's place.'

'That's just what I was thinking,' grunted Bret thought-fully. 'We've used up all or our tricks. To be plain honest, more of them escaped the blast than I'd figured on.' He reached a sudden decision. 'Think you can get the rest of the boys together and head back for Nolan's ranch? There'll be more cover over there and you ought to be able to hold them off, at least until dawn. Somehow, I doubt whether they'll keep up the attack in broad daylight.'

'What about you, Bret?' The other's face was a pale grey blur in the moonlight and it was difficult to make out any expression on it. 'You're not figgering on staying here by yourself, are you? You'd never stand a chance.'

'Mebbe not,' smiled Bret grimly. 'But somebody has to hold this pass until you get clear. Don't worry about me. If things get too hot here I'll be able to slip away into the darkness. Now get going before they beat you to the punch. They aren't going to stay under cover out there much longer.'

The other hesitated for a moment, opened his mouth as if to make another protest, then seemed to realize that it would be futile, that Bret had already made up his mind and nothing would sway him from his purpose. Swiftly, he slithered away into the shadows of the rocks. Bret inched himself forward to where he could see the whole of the trail spread out below him. The rocks which had been torn out by the exploding dynamite had completely blocked the trail at this particular point and he saw, with a sense of satisfaction, that the cluster of rocks were he lay formed a natural strongpoint from which he could see in all directions. Anyone trying to sneak up on him would have to show himself in the open long before he came within shooting distance, unless they used a rifle.

A few minutes later he heard the dull, muffled thunder of horses to his right and he knew that the others were riding out. If the gunhawks heard it too, they gave no sign of it. Bret waited grimly for them to show themselves. If they intended to rush him in a bunch, things could become dangerous; but if they tried to sneak up on him, a few at a time, he ought to be able to pick them off, one by one. Luckily, if they came at him from the direction of the trail, they would have the full moon in their faces.

They did not keep him waiting long. As they rose up out of the rocks on the far side of the blocked trail, Bret knew with a quiet certainty that they were not sure where he was, or even if anyone had remained behind when the main force had ridden out. But they were cautious. No longer did they seem to be as confident as they had been when they had ridden in over the rise.

He allowed them to get within twenty yards of his hiding place before sighting on the leading men, firing methodically, taking careful aim. The first man, stumbling on top of the rise, arched his back as the bullet hit him, blundered blindly forward for five or six feet before falling on to the trail below. The other gunhawks began firing instinctively and bullets hummed and shrieked among the rocks around him. Bret fired again, his face completely devoid of any expression, each shot finding its mark. The Lazy V men had to cross the trail to reach him from that direction and to do so they would be forced to show themselves for over a minute as they scrambled down the steep slope and across the floor of the trail twenty or thirty feet away. There was little doubt that they had recognized the danger of their position and were clearly reluctant to advance.

Bret lifted his head cautiously. A movement to his right caught his attention. It came from between two piles of rocks a little way behind him. Screwing up his eyes against the glare of the moonlight, he made out the black, flat-topped hat rising slowly from among the rocks. Bret paused for a moment. If that gunhawk knew what he was doing, there would be a stick underneath that hat and not a man's head and the killer would be merely waiting for the flash of his guns to give away his exact position.

After a moment, as if the man were satisfied, the hat was withdrawn, the gunman apparently convinced that he had not been spotted and a second later, Bret saw the man clearly as he edged himself forward between two large boulders. This time Bret made no mistake. The man gave a thin scream as Bret fired, and pitched forward into the darkness, rolling down the slope with a bullet in his chest. There was no answering fire from that direction and the man had obviously been moving up alone in an attempt to outflank him.

Rightly surmising that this move had been merely a feint, a ruse to draw his fire and attention away from what was happening in front of him, Bret snapped a quick look along the trail. They were getting ready to rush him this time, spreading themselves out in a loose line across the far ridge. It would be sheer suicide for him to remain there any longer, he decided. He might be able to kill a handful of men before they reached the cover at the bottom of the trail, but the others would be bound to get him. Cautiously, keeping his head low, he edged back, out of the rocks, into the hackberry trees which lay on the far ridge, then ran swiftly through the dim greenness until he came out in the open again. The stallion was still there, loosely tethered to one of the low branches. Swiftly, Bret hit leather and headed away from the scene. Behind him, he heard faint shouts, men yelling orders, and knew that they had heard him go. He gave the stallion its head, felt the powerful surge of muscles as it carried him away over the smooth pasture.

How many men were still there, behind him, it had been impossible to guess with any degree of accuracy. Possibly ten or even twelve, he figured. But that meant, without any shadow of doubt, that the main body of the Lazy V men had taken off in the opposite direction, were possibly already outside the Nolan ranch. The thought was a beating urgency, pounding through his brain. There were still almost five hours to dawn, five hours during which they had to hold off more than twice their numbers of professional killers.

For a long while, there was no sound but the pounding hoofs of the horse beneath him and the keen night wind in his ears. Nolan's spread was if anything larger than Redden's and more than once, he had the feeling that perhaps he had lost his way, taken the wrong direction after leaving the trail. In the moonlight, everything looked the same. He forded a narrow stream, paused for a moment to glance about him, listening for the sound of gunfire which would be the one thing to lead him to the ranch. He had no doubt that the others were there by now, that gunplay had already started.

But he rode for close on another mile before he heard it, faint and distant, somewhere over to his right. Wheeling the stallion, he headed swiftly towards it, eyes peering ahead of him until he made out the ranch house, at the bottom of a gentle slope, nestling among a ring of trees. He tightened his lips thinly. Those trees were a nuisance now. They afforded excellent cover to the gunmen surrounding the ranch. From their shelter, they would be able to take up any position they wished, fire into the house from any direction, from behind cover almost as good and secure as the walls of the house itself.

Close by the house, to the north, Nolan had a field of oats. Now they were burning furiously, fanned by the wind, the stalks as dry as timber after the spell of hot, dry weather. Fortunately, the wind was driving them away from the house, otherwise the men inside would soon be burned out, into the waiting guns of the Lazy V riders.

Dismounting, he crept swiftly down the slope until he was less than twenty yards from the ring of trees. The crash of gunfire rang in his ears as he went to ground with the trained ease of a frontiersman. So far, he had been unseen, but pretty soon, the rest of the riders would come on to the scene and if he did not manage to slip through this screen of men, they would have him trapped. There was little hope of stampeding these men as he had a few nights earlier back at the Redden place. They would not fall for the same trick twice. Somehow, he had to break through them and join the others inside the house. He pursed his lips as he glanced about him. That wasn't going to be too easy, he told himself. Even if he did get through unseen, keen eyes from the ranch would spot him and shoot him down on sight. He didn't relish the idea of being shot at by the men he had come here to help.

Judging by the volume of fire from the direction of the ranch, Nolan and Redden had several men with them. Above the sharp crackle of six-gun fire, he heard the occasional savage, deeper bark of a high-powered rifle. Certainly, the Lazy V men were not having it all their own way this time. He crawled forward until he entered the trees. Darkness closed about him, abruptly. It was like stepping over the dividing line between night and day, going out of the flooding moonlight. Ten yards in front of him he found something which was not natural to the undergrowth. The man lay slumped across the bole of a tree, his hat off and his arms outflung. His legs were twisted beneath him in an unnatural position and even in the green dimness, Bret was able to see the stain of blood on his shirt.

From close at hand, he could hear the rest of the outlaws, talking among themselves, crashing through the undergrowth as they tried to work their way around the ranch. If they kept up this volume of fire, he thought grimly, they would soon be out of ammunition.

With a cat-like stealth, Bret moved through the trees. The gunmen were making so much noise themselves, that it would have been impossible for them to have heard him. Once, he had a nasty moment, when two dark shapes loomed up out of the trees and moved towards him. Swiftly, he flattened himself against the trunk of a tall pine, holding his breath. They came abreast of him, then moved on, totally unaware of his presence. Clearly they had no knowledge of woodcraft.

Breaking out of the trees, he found himself facing the barns. The flickering flames which were racing across the field of oats lit up the sky on the far side of the ranch.

There were still more than forty yards to go, forty yards across open ground and he could not yell out to let those inside the ranch house know who he was, for to have done that would have brought down a hail of accurate fire from the men among the trees and he would have been killed before he had gone more than a dozen paces. Everything now depended upon his stealth and his knowledge of woodcraft. Swiftly, he slipped down on to his stomach and wriggled forward through the tall grass, the stalks not so much as waving as he slithered forward like a snake. Several times, he heard the quiet, vicious hum of slugs biting through the air over his head, but he knew instinctively that they were not meant for him, but for the men in the trees. He could hear movement behind him among the trees, sudden shouting and the beat of horses' hoofs. The rest of the men must have arrived from the trail. Pretty soon, Wicker would know that he had escaped from the trap back there and was somewhere close at hand. It was imperative that he should get under cover before they started looking for him in earnest.

It was a slow and painful process, moving forward on his belly like this. Not until he reached within five feet of the barn did he pause, suck in a deep breath and then launch himself forward. Gratefully, he sank down on to the soft straw, heaving air into his lungs. For the moment, he was safe. Swiftly, he took up his position close to the half-open door of the barn. From there, he could make out the stabbing orange flashes of the guns as the gunhawks continued to fire from the trees.

Answering flashes came from the windows of the ranch. Grimly, Bret waited. For several minutes, the firing continued, then at the corner of his eye, he saw the sudden movement among the trees, the darker patch as a handful of men ran into the open, their heads low, shoulders hunched forward. Several seconds fled before he realized that they were making for the barn where he crouched. He began firing swiftly, both guns in his hands. Three men dropped before the others realized where the fire was coming from. The others flopped down out of sight in the tall grass. They would be more cautious now, would lie there until they plucked up sufficient courage to get to their feet again and try to rush him.

He reloaded the guns, checked them automatically, then leaned his back against the door, eyes alert, body tensed as he waited for them to come on once more. Behind the concealed men, like sparks on the wind, gunfire flared redly among the trees. The minutes began to lengthen. The moon was now bright, high in the sky, flooding the whole scene with yellow light. Bret could hear the men in the tall grass muttering among themselves, but they seemed reluctant to come out into the open again and face his guns. They were equally reluctant to try to get back into the cover of the trees some twenty yards behind him.

Licking his lips, Bret screwed up his eyes against the moonlight, keeping his gaze fixed on the spot where the men had gone to earth. Very soon, they would have to make their move, he decided, and his fingers tightened on the triggers of the guns in reflex action. When they finally made their move, three men stumbled forward, firing from the hip, while the others remained crouched down, out of sight, firing swiftly and accurately at the barn, hoping to force him to keep his head down while the others rushed him.

Savagely, he fired, swinging the guns slightly in a short arc as the three men tried to spread out, bobbing and weaving to present more difficult targets. One fell, clutching at the man who ran next to him, half-dragging him to his knees as he dropped. Even as he hit the ground, the wounded man continued to fire. Bret shot him again and he rolled over and lay still. The other two got to within ten yards of the barn before he shot them. Swiftly, he reloaded the Colts once more. The other men, in the grass, did not relish the idea of coming out into the open now and had stopped firing. Further to his right, he could still hear the crash of firearms. The attackers seemed to have been re-organized and were spreading out to surround the place completely, thereby forcing the men inside to spread their fire. Bret waited until he was certain that the men in the grass did not intend to make any further move, then pushed himself slowly to his feet, threw a swift glance in both directions, and darted swiftly along the front of the barn and towards the house. He had to take a chance here, the chance that those inside the house now knew who he was, had seen the fire coming from the barn.

He reached the rear entrance to the ranch house, whis-tled softly. A moment later, Redden's voice said hoarsely: 'That you, Bret?' The door opened even before he answered and he slipped inside.

'Thought I heard you firing out there from the barn,' said the other tightly. 'At first I wasn't sure, but when I saw those three men drop a couple of minutes ago, I knew I had to be right. Are there many of them still alive?'

'Enough to make trouble,' said Bret grimly. 'How are things going here? Many casualties?'

'One of Nolan's men has been killed and two more wounded, but they can still handle a gun. We're all right for ammunition.'

Bret nodded. 'They're trying to surround the house. When they've done that, they'll probably rush the place and hope to overwhelm us by sheer weight of numbers. They know that by doing that, they'll be able to reduce the effectiveness of our fire.'

'What about that field of oats? We saw them fire it. Think the wind will blow the flames this way?'

'I doubt it. Besides, there's a ten-yard gap between it

and the house. It ought to burn itself out in an hour, mebbe less. But it has one advantage as far as we're concerned. It means that those gunhawks won't be able to attack us from that particular direction, unless they want to be fried alive. We need only keep one man on that side of the house just in case they try to move in along the wall.'

'Cameron is there already,' nodded Redden. He went quickly to the window and glanced out, lips tight. 'Looks as though they're getting ready for another attack on this side. There's a bunch of them on the edge of the wood.'

Bret glanced round, saw Nolan standing there a rifle in his hands. He came forward into the middle of the room. 'Glad to see that you managed to get back here,' he said quietly: 'But that was a fool thing you did back there, trying to hold that trail by yourself. You were godamned lucky that you weren't shot by mistake coming here too.'

Bret grinned at him. 'I think that pretty soon, Wicker is going to realize that he's losing far too many men to be able to keep up his attack. Even though it means losing face as far as the people of Sundown are concerned, he'll have to call it off before long. He must have lost almost half of his fighting force. Any more casualties, and he'll have trouble from the other ranchers and homesteaders. I've seen this kind of situation before, many times. If the iron hand falters, the oppressed aren't long in rising and taking the law into their own hands; and as far as Darby Wicker is concerned, that means either a rope or a bullet.'

'I only hope to God you're right' muttered the other. There was the wild shriek of a bullet hitting the wall of the house outside wailing off into the distance. 'But for the moment they don't seem inclined to give up the attack.'

He went out of the room and Bret took up his position alongside Redden by the window. Outside in the moonlight it was almost as clear as day. A dozen or so men were massing in front of the trees and Bret thought that he saw the stocky figure of Darby Wicker among them urging them on but he couldn't be sure and he knew from past experience that the moonlight was inclined to play tricks with one's vision.

'Here they come again' murmured Redden quietly out of the corner of his mouth. He brought up his gun and fired three times in rapid succession. One of the men running down the slope seemed to lose his footing and pitched forward rolling over and over until he reached the bottom. Only when he lay still and did not rise did Bret realize that the rancher's bullets had found their mark. The other gunhawks came forward in a blundering rush yelling fiercely at the tops of their voices firing as they came.

Carefully taking deliberate aim Bret picked them off, coolly one by one. This was not fair fighting as he had always known it. This was little short of massacre. The men out there in the moonlight running blindly forward stood very little chance of survival. But they continued to come on in spite of this. Some reached the bottom of the slope and went down behind what little cover they could find. Four of them crouched down behind the watering trough in the centre of the yard showing their heads occasionally whenever they snapped a shot in the direction of the ranch.

Twenty minutes later they ran back towards the trees followed by several shots. One man was hit before he could reach cover and his companions dragged him the rest of the way but from the way he sagged among them Bret guessed that taking him back had been more of a gesture than anything.

Gradually the firing died down. There was silence among the trees and the moon dipped past its zenith and lowered itself towards the western horizon. The stars began to pale as the dawn brightened in the east. The trees stood out in stark relief against the skyline. From somewhere in the distance Bret heard the sharp snicker of a horse. He rubbed his stubbled chin and realized just how weary and hungry he really was.

Redden must have been feeling the same way for he stirred himself and said hoarsely: 'What the hell do you reckon they're doing out there Bret?'

'Probably debating whether it's worth their while to try one last all-out assault against us. If they do then it'll come pretty soon before full daylight. If not they'll pull out and my guess is that Wicker will send for more of his half-breed killers from over the border.'

The other's lips quirked into a grimace. 'If he does that then we're finished Bret. Make no mistake about that. We wouldn't stand a chance against an army of half-breed Mexicans.'

'I know' Bret nodded easily. 'That's what's been worrying me for the past three days. I've been trying to think out some plan of stopping him from sending word. It means that someone will have to watch that trail to the border and see to it that none of Wicker's boys gets through.'

The other eyed him sharply for a long moment then gave a quick nod. 'Think you can keep a watch on this side of the ranch while I go and rustle up some food for us?' he asked. 'Most of the boys will be hungry and dead beat by sun-up.'

Bret nodded. 'Sure thing' he replied. He eased his tired body into a more comfortable position balancing the guns in his hands. 'We ought to get plenty of warning whatever they decide to do.'

The other went out of the room leaving the door open behind him. With an effort Bret forced his eyes to remain open. Still no sound from the trees overlooking the ranch. Meanwhile the daylight was getting stronger every minute and he guessed that the sun would be up within a quarter of an hour. Any chance the gunhawks had of taking them by surprise was gone now. They would be seen the moment they burst out of the trees.

It was ten minutes later when he spotted the sudden movement and saw Wicker stride out into the open almost contemptuously. The other's voice reached him easily: 'Don't think that you've beaten me, Nolan' he yelled. 'I'll be coming back and the next time I'll have so many men with me that we'll overrun your place completely.'

Someone inside one of the other rooms fired once. The bullet missed but must have passed sufficiently close to the other to make him duck swiftly. A second later the man had vanished into the trees and the unmistakable sound of horses moving away could be clearly heard.

Bret relaxed. There was always the possibility that this was nothing more than an old Indian trick to lure them out into the open but he didn't think so. Wicker had lost too many men with this night's work. If he was to maintain his position as the big Boss of the surrounding territory he would need more men to help him. He would bide his time until the killers from over the Mexican border arrived and then take his revenge for this defeat.

Half an hour later Bret was drinking coffee and eating a sumptuous breakfast with the rest of the men. Two of the ranch hands had ridden to the rise overlooking the pasture land beyond the trees and had returned with the news that there was no sign of the Lazy V gunhawks although several of their dead were lying in the underbrush among the trees.

'Well Bret,' said Redden after a short pause, 'what do you make of it? Think he's given up his attempt for the time being or will he strike again when he figgers that we're not expecting it?'

Bret shook his head. 'I don't think he'll do that. He's been beaten twice and beaten decisively. He won't dare to run that risk again. The people in Sundown and the rest of the ranchers not to mention the homesteaders are all watching this feud with interest. They'll back the side which they reckon stands the best chance of winning. At the moment that isn't Darby Wicker. For the first time in his career, he's on the losing side. He has to wait for reinforcements before he can attack again.'

'So he's going to send a man, possibly two men across the border to send word that he needs men. And he can pay them well. They'll come,' declared Nolan tightly. He sipped his coffee. 'How do you propose to deal with that little problem? We can expect no real help from Fort Laramie, I assure you. Even if these men enter the state illegally.'

'I know. It's pity that the Government was so short-sighted in its policy that it withdrew those troops so soon. We certainly need them around now. Even these Mexican killers might think twice about fighting, if they found themselves facing seasoned troops with a few heavy guns.'

'G'darn it,' muttered Redden, 'you'd think the Government ought to be able to afford us some protection against men like Wicker.'

'He's too clever. They'll never be able to pin anything on him, I'm afraid. He'll have an alibi for anything. There are too many men ready to swear that we're in the wrong.'

'So you figger that the only thing to do now is to watch the Mexico trail and stop Wicker's men before they can get through.'

'Yes. At least, if we can do that, it ought to give us a little breathing space in which to formulate some other plans.' He finished his coffee, then got to his feet. 'In the mean-time, I'd better take a look at those two wounded men. I'm not much of a doctor, I'm afraid, but in the circumstances, I doubt if you would get one out here from Sundown.'

'That drunken old reprobate wouldn't be much good anyway,' said Redden emphatically. 'I reckon these men stand a better chance of survival with you than they do with him.'

'You flatter me,' said Bret. But inwardly, he felt a warm glow of pleasure. Going into the room, he found the two men stretched out, one of them on the low couch, the other on the table. Both had been hit in the shoulder, in one case the bullet had smashed its way out through the back and it only remained to clean the wound and plug it.

The other man was in a worse condition. The bullet was still there, lodged in the vicinity of the right lung and he had to probe for it for several minutes before he succeeded in extracting it. At last, he was satisfied that he had done all he could for the two men.

4

Owlhoot Trail

Bret was out on the range again after less than four hours' sleep. He woke feeling refreshed and rode swiftly from the Nolan spread on to the trail which wound between Redden's place and the desert which stretched to the east of Sundown. If Wicker sent any of his men south to the border, this was the way he would come. Wicker would undoubtedly want those men in a hurry and would order his men to take the shortest possible route into Mexico. Even at the best of times, it would be a four days' journey.

To his left, the sunlight glittered on the sluggish water of the wide river, but he skirted this and cut into the desert. This was a barren and inhospitable country and if a man lost himself here, with the wind blowing the sand from the east, obliterating his tracks in an hour, he could wander around for days until he died from thirst. Even now, the sun was a burning disc in the sullen sky and the heat struck with a searing force though his shirt, burning his back and shoulders.

He recalled the last time he had ridden across this desert a few days earlier heading for Sundown. Then it had seemed that his long quest was almost at an end, that nothing stood between him and what he had sworn to do. But killing Darby Wicker had not proved to be the simple thing he had anticipated then. Now, he was caught up in a web of range-wars and feuds, of intrigue and corruption. Somehow, he had to find a way out of it, but unless he stopped Wicker getting word to the Mexican bandits who would undoubtedly throw in their lot with him, everything would be finished, not only for the ranchers and decent people of the territory, but for him too. He no longer doubted that Wicker knew he was there and he would also know the reason why he had come. As he rode though the sand, he allowed his mind to drift back into the past, several years before. The war was still in progress; a long and bitter fight in which families had been split, in which brother fought brother and father fought son. Those had been terrible days, but even so, they had fought cleanly. There had, however, been men to whom the laws of war meant nothing. Men who fought in the uniform of the Confederate Army, but who thought of nothing but plunder and murder; men who fought only for gain and profit and who were disowned by both sides.

Such men as those who rode with Lane and Quantrill, sacking the small Kansas towns along the Missouri border, putting whole populations to the sword. His lips tightened convulsively with the memory of those days. These undisciplined brigades of freebooters had stopped at nothing, had shown no mercy to men or innocent women and children. For them, the war had merely been an excuse to kill and destroy.

Darby Wicker had been one of the men who had ridden with Quantrill. A vicious killer who murdered for the sheer, sadistic delight of it. It was after one of these raids, that on Lawrence in August 1863, that Bret had returned there after a spell of duty in the field, only to find that his parents, his sister and younger brother had been mercilessly put to death in the most horrible way imaginable by these men and that, according to the few eye-witness reports he had been able to get, it had been Darby Wicker, one of the leaders of the Quantrill band, who had been directly responsible. Ever since that day, he had sworn that Wicker would pay for that act with his life. Now he was closer to fulfilling that vow than at any other time since the war had ended and he had been free to look for this vicious killer. He wondered how many of the people in Sundown were aware of the true nature of the snake they harboured in their midst. Very few of them, he felt sure. Now, so long after the war, it was not the sort of thing of which any man, even Darby Wicker, could be justly proud. It was something he would keep to himself, a closely guarded secret, for it was just possible that there might come a time, some time in the future, when events began to catch up with him, when he would no longer be able to hide behind the band of trained killers he had hired, both for his own protection and to carry out his orders. Then, if it were known who he really was and what he had done, retribution would be both swift and sure.

Bret reined his horse at one of the waterholes and allowed it to drink. He drank deeply from his water bottle, then dismounted and filled it from the water. It tasted warm and brackish, but it went down and stayed down, slaking his thirst.

Darby Wicker had ridden back to the Lazy V ranch after his failure to take the Nolan spread. There was a deep anger within him, and a rising urgency which he could scarcely contain. If he allowed these ranchers to get away with this, he thought savagely, as he reined his horse, slid out of the saddle, and handed it to the groom who came forward to meet him, it would not be long before the empire which he had built up around Sundown over the past seven years, began to disintegrate in front of his eyes. He knew now, without a shadow of a doubt, who was at the back of it all. He had thought that somehow, he had succeeded in shaking Bret Manders off his trail, but now he knew he had been wrong. The other had located him again and he would have to be stopped before he did any more damage to the plans he had in mind for this territory.

While the rest of the men went off to the bunkhouse, taking the wounded with them, he called Bart Williams, the foreman of the ranch, into the house. He was no longer so confident that he could defeat these people with the few men he had available. After these last two beatings which they had taken at the hands of Manders and the ranchers, he had the impression that his men were no longer so full of fight, they did not have the stomach to go out again and take another licking. No longer did he have much faith in these fighting men if they met with any further determined opposition. Deep down inside, Wicker was a realist and he recognized that, somehow, Manders had succeeded in infusing some courage and determination into these men who, previously, had been like sheep. Whenever he had offered them a price for their land, they had either taken it or been run out of the territory. Now they were standing up to him and this was something which he neither liked, nor intended to continue.

'You wanted to see me, Boss.' Williams came into the room and stood just inside the door. He was a tall, red-faced *hombre* with high cheek-bones which testified to some Spanish ancestry in spite of his name.

Wicker nodded his head heavily. 'I need someone to do a little job for me,' he said thickly. 'It's important and at the moment, there aren't many of the men I can really trust.'

'You're thinking of sending me.' There was no question in the other's tone. Rather it was a statement of fact.

'That's right. It's quite obvious that the rest of the boys have little stomach for a real showdown after what has happened during the last two raids on the ranches. I've got to have men I can really trust. There's one other point that has been worrying me all day. How come those *hombres* knew where we were going to attack and when?' He lowered himself into the chair in front of the empty hearth and watched the foreman from beneath lowered lids. There was something faintly accusing in that calm,

steady gaze and the other was acutely aware of it. He said
suddenly, sharply: 'Don't look at me like that, Boss. It was
nothing to do with me. But it seems clear that somebody
has talked. You reckon it might have been the sheriff. This
guy Manders was parleying with him yesterday morning,
and that yeller-livered coyote would sell his soul to the
devil if he thought he could get away with it.'

'That possibility has crossed my mind,' said Wicker
smoothly. 'But somehow, I don't think it's the right one.
Veldon is a coward at heart. He knows that if he ever
double-crossed me, he'd pay for it with his life, and he
wouldn't die easily. No, I don't think he talked, but we'd
better make sure. I'll get him over here and question him.
It won't be difficult to tell if he's lying. And if he is —' He
deliberately allowed the remainder of his sentence to
remain unsaid, but the threat hung quivering on the air
for several moments.

'Is that what you want me to do, Boss?' asked the other,
after a brief pause. 'Bring in the sheriff?'

'No. I've something more important for you to do. I
want you to saddle up as soon as possible and head across
the Mexican border. I think you can understand why.'

'Sure, Boss. I get you. I get in touch with Gonzales.
He'll come with his band and we finish off those ranchers
once and for all.'

Wicker laughed harshly. 'Exactly. I think our friend,
Bret Manders is in for a distinctly unpleasant surprise.
How long will it take you to get to Gonzales and get back
here?'

The other pursed his lips, face drawn up into a scowl.
'The best part of seven days' hard riding,' he said at last.

Wicker nodded. 'Go to it,' he ordered. 'And don't
come back here without him. Tell Gonzales that I shall pay
him well. He'll understand.'

'I get you, Boss,' grinned the other mirthlessly. 'Deal
me in when you ride again. I've got a score to settle with
this *hombre* who calls himself Manders.'

'No.' Wicker's voice was sharp and authoritative. 'He'll be taken alive. I want to see him die.'

The other shrugged. 'If that's the way you want it,' he said thinly.

'That's the way I want it,' echoed Wicker. 'Now pick yourself the fastest horse and get moving.' He waited until the other reached the door, then went on quietly: 'I think I ought to warn you before you leave that Manders isn't a fool. He'll have guessed what's in my mind and he'll be out watching the trail. Take care that he doesn't jump you. It matters little to me whether you get yourself killed or not, but I want that message to get through to Gonzales.'

For a moment, the big foreman's eyes narrowed into mere slits. His large, beefy hands hovered over the guns at his waist. Then he forced a guttural laugh and spun on his heel. 'I'll watch for him, Boss,' he grated quickly. 'But if he does try to jump me, it ain't going to be easy taking him alive.'

'All right, all right. If you have to kill him to get through, then kill him. But not unless it's absolutely neces-sary. I've been waiting to get Bret Manders on the wrong side of a gun for almost eight years. I thought I'd lost him in Arizona, but he must have picked up my trail.' He seemed to be speaking almost to himself, then stirred and glared at the other. 'Well, what the devil are you waiting for? Move.'

The other backed quickly out of the room and strode along the corridor. A moment later, Wicker saw him cross-ing the courtyard in the brilliant sunlight, yelling to one of the grooms for a horse. Wicker watched with a cruel amusement on his face. Inwardly, he hoped that the big foreman did meet up with Manders somewhere along the desert trail. If he did, he felt certain that only one of them would survive. Williams was a fast man with a gun, one of the best – which was the main reason why he had hired him in the first place. That, and the fact that the streak of cruelty in him was enough to keep the rest of the men on the ranch in check. Everyone in the Lazy V gang feared the killer with the clear grey eyes and the quick, ready temper and so far, none of them had ever dared to cross him.

But even so, even though he knew from past experience of the big man's powers with a six-shooter, Wicker was not fooled. He knew that if anything Bret Manders was even faster with a gun and that in fair fight, Williams would get the worst of it. His lips curled into a cruel sneer as he watched the other swing easily into the saddle and ride out.

This way, he was making sure of one of the men who threatened him. He had known for some time now that the big ranch foreman had been talking against him, had been feeling out the rest of the men, hoping perhaps to get them to side with him in a showdown. Now, he thought with satisfaction, at least one of those two men would probably be dead within a day or so. After that, it ought to be relatively simple to deal with the other, whoever it might be.

Half an hour later, he made his way to the bunkhouse. The rest of the hands were already there at chow. They glanced up as he entered and one or two made to get to their feet, but he waved them back and singled out two of them, two shifty-eyed characters he knew he could trust. Neither of them had any liking for the big foreman which all suited his purpose.

'I wanted to see both of you in the house in twenty minutes,' he said softly. 'I've a job for you.'

They nodded in unison and something flickered at the back of their eyes. Wicker waited for a few moments, then made his way back across the courtyard. The chances of Williams getting through along the desert trail, with Bret Manders almost certainly watching, were very slim indeed; and he had never been a man for taking unnecessary chances. It meant that he would have to have a second arrow to his bow and that was something he could do right away.

When the two men arrived, he deliberately kept them standing by the door, their hats in their hands. They looked a little uncomfortable standing there and he knew by the expressions on their swarthy faces that they had racked their brains in an attempt to figure out why he had sent for them. By now, they must have known that Williams had ridden off to the south-east.

'Somebody has to ride out and get word through to Gonzales,' he said after a pause. 'I need men and I need them fast. Tell Gonzales that I want all the men he can spare. There will be plenty of rich pickings for them if they come. These ranchers have got to be stopped now, before they can win the townspeople over on to their side. If they do that, they might be able to run us out of the territory or raise such a shout that the Government will move in.'

'But Williams? We saw him ride off to the south-east,' said one of the men.

Wicker said sharply: 'Williams will be heading into trouble. I think he knows that, but in either case, even if he manages to slip through the cordon these people will put across the trail, that something I can't risk. You'll both ride due south. Keep well away from the desert trail, ride across country until you're well over the frontier. Once there, you ought to find Gonzales within a day or so. Get him and his men here as quickly as you can. Get me?'

'We understand,' grunted the taller of the two men. He hitched his gun-belt a little higher on his hips. 'And if we too run into any trouble?'

'Take care of it,' snapped Wicker. 'But keep this in mind, I don't want you to go out there looking for trouble. All that concerns me at the moment, is getting those men here within six or seven days. After that, you'll get all of the trouble you want. I promise you that.'

The man's thin lips lengthened into a cruel smile. He asked: 'Do you reckon we'll have big trouble from the ranchers and homesteaders, Boss?'

'If we let them have their own way and think that we're

finished – yes. But not if we crush them once and for all.'

'They haven't the guns to stand up and fight in the open,' declared the second man. 'They're no damned good when it comes to fighting.'

'They shot and killed half of our force,' said Wicker, a trace of anger in his voice. 'We've set out twice to fire their ranches and each time we've been sent back with our tails between our legs like so many rats.' His hands, on the back of the tall chair, tightened convulsively, the knuckles whitening under the skin. 'But it isn't going to happen again. Now get moving and — No! Wait a minute.'

He called them back as a fresh thought struck him. Watching them both closely from beneath lowered lids, he asked softly: 'Were any of the men in the Golden Ace saloon yesterday morning? Think now. This could be important.'

'They could have been,' nodded one of the men. 'What's on your mind, Boss?'

'I'm just trying to figger things out. Somehow, Bret Manders and the others must have known about our plans to raid the Nolan place last night.'

'They could have been just plumb lucky,' interrupted the second man. Wicker spun on him and said thinly: 'Don't talk like a fool. It would have taken them the best part of the afternoon to set those booby traps and lay that dynamite along the sides of the trail. They must have known by morning at the latest. That means they were tipped off by someone in Sundown. I happen to know that Manders was in town early yesterday morning, talking with the sheriff.'

'You think he told him?'

'Could be, but I doubt it. There's someone else in town who's been acting as a spy and I intend to find out who it is.' He gave a brief nod. 'But that won't concern you men. Hit the trail and bring back those men.'

Bret camped in the open that night, among the rocks, on a low ridge which overlooked the winding length of the desert trail. It was cold now that the sun had gone down

and the stiff breeze which blew steadily from the west
whipped up the sand and flung it into his face, stinging his
eyes and making it impossible for him to sleep. In a way,
this was a good thing, for he knew with a sudden certainty
that if Wicker did intend sending any messenger through
to the Mexican bandits to the south, then it would be very
soon. He could not afford to waste any more precious
time, now that he was sitting on top of a powder-keg which
threatened to erupt beneath him at any moment. Things
were going to become very hot for Wicker and the Lazy V
hands in Sundown, if only he and the ranchers could get
the townsfolk to fight.

He pulled his blanket more tightly around his neck,
eyes slitted against the sand, staring up at the stars which
glittered brilliantly in the dark velvet night sky. The sand
would muffle the sound of an approaching horse and he
knew that, whatever happened, he would have to remain
awake all night. There was the distinct possibility that
Wicker would guess the trail would be watched and
whoever he sent, would be alert and watchful.

For a moment, he fancied he heard something in the
distance, some sound which he could not identify and he
lifted his head slowly, straining every nerve and sense to
pick out the slightest sound or the faintest movement. But
after a few moments, he felt satisfied that there had been
nothing and lowered his head to the bed-roll again. In
another half hour or so, the moon would come up and he
would be able to see a little more clearly. Already, there
was a faint yellow patch low down against the eastern horizon, beyond the rocks.

It was possible, he thought, turning things over in his
mind as he lay there under the blanket, that the Lazy V
rider was camped a little further back along the trail for
the night. But even as the thought passed through his
mind he dismissed it. That was hardly likely. The man
would have been given strict orders by Darby Wicker to
ride hard and ride fast and not stop for anything until he

was clear over the Mexican border. Wicker needed those men badly, desperately. Until they arrived and threw in their lot with him, he was literally at the mercy of the ranchers and homesteaders, if the latter only knew it. If they could muster their full force and ride on the Lazy V ranch, they could take it with very little trouble and Wicker's evil dominion over the surrounding territory would come to an end overnight. But that was, at the moment, little more than a dream.

The stallion snickered quietly a few feet away, the sound jarring in the stillness of the desert. Bret rolled over on to his side, eyes wide open, waiting for the moon to come up, to give him light. The seconds and the minutes ticked by with a monotonous slowness. There was something oddly weird and uncanny about the desert in the flooding moonlight a little while later. It was virtually impossible to distinguish the narrow trail from the sand on either side, but as he leaned his back against the wall of rock behind him, narrowing his eyes against the sudden glare, he could see that for a couple of miles at least, back in the direction of Sundown, the desert, the trail itself, were empty. Nothing moved out there as he sat with his rifle balanced over his knees.

For close on an hour he watched the trial, watchful and alert. Had he been mistaken when he had anticipated Wicker to send for more help? He was beginning to think that he must have been when he spotted the faint movement in the distance, too far away to be made out clearly even in the moonlight, but obviously a rider heading in his direction at a fast gallop. The man was in a hurry and did not seem to be too cautious.

Slowly, Bret lifted the rifle from his knees and slid forward, taking cover behind the rocks. The trail, at this point, passed within ten yards of his hiding place and he felt confident that he could drop the other, if it turned out to be one of Wicker's men, before he had a chance to draw.

As the other approached, he noticed that the man had

slowed his mount, was moving forward more carefully now. The reason was immediately obvious and strengthened Bret's conviction that this was one of the Lazy V riders. While he had been out there in the open, there had been no need for caution. The other would have been able to see for several miles and there had been no point in slowing his horse. Now, as he approached the high ridges which bunched together on either side of the trail, there was need for caution.

A quarter of a mile away, the other reined his mount and slithered out of the saddle. Bret watched through narrowed eyes as the man bent, obviously searching the trail for something. Then realization came to Bret in a single instant. The other knew that someone would be watching the trail and was trying to pick out his tracks. He tightened his lips into a grim line as he peered through the crack between two rough-edged boulders. Things were not going to be as simple as he had imagined. Whoever that was down there, he was an experienced frontiersman like himself, and it was highly improbable that he would ride into a trap.

The man led his mount forward by the bridle for a little way, then ducked into the cover of the rocks immediately ahead of him, leaving the horse out on the trail. Bret cursed softly under his breath. The other was only guessing, but he would circle around the knot of boulders overlooking the trail and try to sneak up on the position from behind, just on the off-chance that someone was hiding there, watching for him.

Very carefully, he lifted his head, straining his eyes to try to pick out the other, but the man had sneaked into the rocks and was lost to sight; only the horse was visible, out there on the trail, standing apparently unconcerned. Bret felt a tightening of his stomach muscles as he sank back again, scarcely daring to breathe. He ought to have used the rifle and picked the other off before he had had the chance to get under cover. But that would have meant

shooting to kill at a man who might be a completely innocent rider.

There was nothing for it now but to remain where he
was, to wait for the other man to come to him and to beat
him to the draw. For long moments, there was silence all
around him. The Lazy V gunhawk could have been
anywhere among those tumbled rocks which lay etched
with moonlight and shadow all around him. Very
cautiously, he edged forward an inch at a time. Even there,
he could see nothing. The darkness there, where the
moonlight failed to penetrate, was black and complete.

From somewhere across the valley, there came the
eerie, high-pitched wail of a coyote and a little shiver
went up and down Bret's spine. If only the other would
show himself, even for a brief instant, it would be
enough. But clearly the man was taking no chances what-
soever. Bret could hear nothing and he doubted that the
other would be able to move among the rocks without
making some slight sound. He lay with his arms against
the rock, the rifle cocked, ready for use, and waited. He
had lived too long with danger and violent death not to
feel just a little afraid, but he did not allow this fear to
rise up and choke him as it would any lesser man. He
held himself under tight control, knowing that this was a
personal showdown, that it would be either him or the
other man.

Then, quite suddenly, he heard the faint scrape of
booted heels on the smooth rock and he held his head a
little on one side as he tried desperately to judge from
which direction the sound had come. It had been very
faint and fleeting and in the darkness, hearing was the
most deceptive of the senses. A moment later, the sound
came again, a little closer this time and now he knew
almost exactly where the man was. Such was his uncanny
ability to place sounds that he could almost have fired into
the blackness and hit the man, but he held his fire and
waited for the other to come on. If possible, he wanted to

take the other alive. There were a lot of questions which could be answered if he succeeded in getting this man back to Redden's ranch. True, Fay Saunders could also give them some information, but he didn't want to drag the girl too deeply into this affair.

If Wicker discovered that the girl was helping them, she could expect no mercy from him. He would kill her with as little compunction as he had killed any of the ranchers or their men; with as little mercy as when he had killed Bret's own parents and sister back in Lawrence in the final days of the war.

Keeping his body inside the shadows thrown by the rocks, he stiffened for a moment as he caught his first glimpse of the man. The other had his rifle over his shoulders and was working his way up the steep face of the ledge. It would be a hard and tortuous climb, Bret knew, having surveyed that side of the ledge before dark, and clearly the other was relying on taking him by surprise, by advancing from the least likely direction. Bret smiled grimly to himself in the darkness as he eased the barrel of his rifle forward.

Not until the other had pulled himself over the edge of the rocky ledge and lay panting faintly in the shadows, less than ten yards away, did he say in a quiet, faintly derisive voice: 'Hold it there, mister and don't try to go for that rifle.'

He heard the sharp intake of breath as the other lifted his head suddenly. He could see the man's face as a pale blur in the dimness and noticed that his hands were flat against the rock, his arms stretched out almost to their fullest extent. The other lay still, not moving a muscle.

'That's better,' Bret climbed slowly to his feet. 'Just stay there, otherwise this rifle might go off.'

He reached the other in a couple of strides, pulled the rifle from the man's hands and tossed it over the side of the ledge. It crashed on to the rocks several feet below. Stooping again, he relieved the other of his guns, then ordered him to get to his feet and stand against the rocky wall.

'What is this?' snarled the other savagely as he got his breath back. He stood glaring at Bret through slitted eyes. 'A hold-up? If it is, then you're wasting your time. You'll get nothing from me.'

'Don't try to bluff me,' snapped Bret. 'I'm in no mood for that. I know exactly who you are and what you're doing here.'

'Yeah. Suppose you tell me.' The other still seemed determined to try to bluff it out with him.

'Right, I will. You're one of the Lazy V hands. Darby Wicker sent you to cross the border for some of those Mexican bandits to the south. He needs those men to help him crush the ranchers around Sundown. But he also warned you that the trail might be watched, so you decided to take no chances. That's why you slipped off your mount and climbed the rocks back there, hoping to get me in the back. Somehow, I doubt whether Wicker will like this, if he hears of it.'

'You don't know what you're talking about,' muttered the other sullenly. 'I don't know any guy by the name of Wicker. I'm riding from Sundown and heading for Fort Laramie. I got a friend there with the military.'

'Sure.' Bret nodded. 'Then why go to all that trouble to climb the rocks when you could have kept on riding?'

The other said nothing but simply stared at him with an expression of anger on his face and naked hatred staring out of his close-set eyes.

'I thought so,' Bret nodded again. He motioned the other to move. 'We'd better be getting back.'

'Back?' There was a note of surprise in the man's gruff voice. 'You ain't taking me back to Sundown?' Was there alarm too in his tone? Bret wasn't sure.

'Afraid of what Wicker might do to you if he finds out what happened?' said Bret quietly. 'I'm afraid he might decide that you're no longer of any use to him.' He decided to play on the other's fear for a little while longer. That way, it was possible that the other might talk.

'OK. So I'm foreman at the Lazy V ranch,' growled the other. 'But that ain't no cause for you to hold me up like this and force me to go back with you into Sundown.'

'Nobody said you were going back into Sundown,' said Bret meaningly. He followed the other along the narrow trail, down through the clustered rocks and boulders, on to the flatness of the desert trail. The man turned abruptly and there was a sudden look of unmistakable fear on his broad, fleshy face.

'You're not handing me over to the ranchers,' he gasped. 'G'darn it, you can't do that. There'd be a lynching.'

'It's no better than you deserve,' muttered Bret, urging him towards the waiting horse. 'If they do decide to lynch you when they've finished, I'm not going to stop 'em.'

'But you're the law, ain't you.' The other seemed definitely frightened now he was in the hands of the men he had tried to destroy. 'You've gotta give a man a fair trial. I was only taking orders from Wicker. If I hadn't carried them out, he would have killed me.'

'Mebbe so.' Bret whistled for his own mount while the other climbed into the saddle. He was still watchful for trickery on the other's part, but he doubted if the man would try to make a break for it, not with a rifle trained on him, and Bret had made it clear to him that he would shoot him the minute he tried anything funny.

Pulling himself up into the saddle, he rested the rifle on the pommel and looked across at the other. 'You've got a hell of a lot to answer for, but I guess you'll get a fair trial if you co-operate. We're going to stop Wicker and stop him good. The sooner you realize that, the better. He won't be able to help you now. Without those men from across the border it'll be an easy matter to wipe him out, to give him a taste of his medicine. The townsfolk are beginning to get wise to him, they've suffered under him for long enough. Wouldn't surprise me if there ain't a hanging coming up soon.'

Slowly, they rode back along the trail. There were still close on fifteen miles to go before they reached Redden's spread, but Bret was banking on Wicker keeping his men on the Lazy V ranch in case of trouble. He doubted if the other would have any men coming out to watch the trails leading into Sundown.

The moon went down and the dawn brightened, while they were still the best part of ten miles from their objective. The heat began to grow in intensity. The horses slowed their pace, their heads hanging a little. The gunhawk wiped his forehead with the back of his hand. 'Can't we rest up a while, Manders?' he asked hoarsely. 'I'm almost beat.'

'We'll rest at the next waterhole,' said Bret, alert for trickery. 'Until then we keep moving, and don't try anything. Just remember that there's a rifle trained on you every minute and I won't hesitate to use it. So don't twitch an eyelid if you want to stay alive.'

They reached the waterhole a little before noon. The sun was blazing down on them from the cloudless sky, a glaring, copper-coloured disc which seemed to burn the desert fiercely all around them, forcing all of the colour out of it, until there was only the bright yellow-white blankness that hurt the eyes and the shimmering heat waves that shocked up at them from all sides.

'All right,' ordered Bret harshly. 'Get down and fill your water-bottle. And no tricks, mind.'

He sat easily in the saddle while the other dismounted, went over to the waterhole and dipped in his bottle. After slaking his thirst, the other said throatily. 'I thought you said we'd rest up a little while, here, Manders.'

Bret nodded, pushed the rifle into its leather holster along the saddle and dropped nimbly to the ground. He saw the other's hard eyes fasten on the guns in their holsters, saw the sudden cunning expression in the man's eyes and knew instinctively what he was thinking.

'Better not try it,' he said softly. 'I don't particularly want to kill you, but if you make any wrong move, then I will.'

The other lapsed into moody silence, his legs doubled beneath him as he screwed on the cap of his water bottle. The wind had died down completely now and the heat increased, soaking through their shirts, sapping the moisture through their clothing. Bret felt his eyes begin to lid and close and forced himself to remain awake. He had had only three hours sleep in the past seventy-two hours and he knew that he could not remain fully alert much longer. He had to get this man back to the Redden ranch before he jumped him.

Five minutes later, he hoisted himself to his feet, stood swaying a little then pulled himself upright. 'All right,' he said hoarsely. 'On your feet and let's get started.'

For a moment, it looked as if the other intended to disregard the order. He sat and stared defiantly at Bret, his lips drawn back into a leering grin. 'You ain't had much sleep for the past few days, have you, Manders?' he said softly. 'Ain't no sense in denying it. I figgered that out long ago. You'd never have had a chance of spotting me last night if you hadn't stayed awake all the time. And if you were one of those back at the Nolan place when we attacked, you couldn't have had any sleep then either. You must be pretty tired by now.' The grin widened. 'You've only got to relax once, Manders, just one second when you ain't as watchful and it'll be the finish for you.'

'Get on your horse and keep riding,' snapped Bret. His hands hovered close to the guns at his waist. 'If you so much as bat an eyelid, I'll drill you. Mebbe you do have information that we could use against Wicker, but that ain't going to stop me from shooting you. Just remember that if you ever get any wrong ideas.'

'Sure, I'll remember,' drawled the other. He got slowly

to his feet and stood looking at Bret for a long moment, then turned to move towards his horse. It was at that moment, just as he was turning away that he kicked savagely at the sand with the heel of his right boot, sending it into Bret's face, stinging his eyes. Instinctively, Bret staggered back, shaking his head, trying to blink the blinding, irritating grains out of his eyes.

With a wild oath, the other hurled himself forward, one beefy fist lashing into Bret's face. Acting more by instinct than anything else, Bret aimed a savage blow with his bunched fist at the blurred face in front of him. He seemed to be seeing things through a shifting curtain of crimson and he knew that the other had also managed things so that he had the sun shining directly in his eyes.

More by luck than judgement his fist caught the other just as he was moving in, confident that he had Bret at his mercy, that he could finish the fight with one blow before Bret could reach for his guns. The gunhawk's head snapped back on his shoulders as he reeled under the force of the blow. Even as he fell back, Bret tried to rub the sand out of his eyes. They still stung badly, but it was now possible for him to see out of them. The other was just pushing himself to his feet, mouth working, arms swinging loosely as he stepped forward for the kill. There was no time for Bret to draw his guns and with the man so close, it would be difficult to be sure of killing him outright. Besides, something at the back of his mind urged him to take the other alive if it was at all possible to do so.

He rode the wild, jabbing blow which the other aimed for his head, sucking air down into his lungs as he feinted to the right, then lashed at the face in front of him. The gunhawk took the blow with a roar of animal-like rage and continued to come in, throwing caution to the winds, his one object to strangle Bret and get his hands on the guns in their holsters.

Swiftly, completely on balance again, Bret hammered at the other, blow after blow, striking him on the face and body. Blood oozed from the other's burst lip and his mouth was thinned into a snarl of defiance, showing the uneven teeth. Bret gathered himself, threw two short piston-like jabs into the man's face, his knuckles grazing the flesh over the high cheek-bones, then put all of his weight behind the right-handed blow which finished flush on the other's jaw. The gunhawk's knees sagged as though unable to bear his weight and he pitched forward on to his face in the sand at Bret's feet.

He was barely conscious, but Bret grabbed him by the shirt and hauled him on to his feet where he stood swaying drunkenly. His face was a battered, bleeding mess, one eye almost closed, his lips split and puffy and a trickle of blood oozing down from the corner of his mouth, across his chin.

'I warned you what would happen if you tried anything,' he said in a husky voice. 'Seems you need to be taught a real lesson before you take anything in.'

He thrust the other away from him, releasing his grip at the same time. The man swayed backwards, eyes glazed, slumped to his knees and lay there for a long moment, sucking air down into his heaving chest. The muscles of his throat were corded and constricted and his mouth worked spasmodically, as if he were trying to say something but the words kept getting themselves lost.

Going over to the waterhole, Bret scooped up some in the man's hat which had fallen off during the fight, then went back and flung it over the other's face. The eyes flickered open as the man stared up at him and for a moment there was no recognition in them. Then, coughing and spluttering, he pushed himself up on to his hands, shaking his head as the water ran into his eyes and mouth.

'G'darn you, Manders, I'll kill you for that,' he snarled.

'Better be careful that I don't kill you first,' said Bret easily, touching the handles of the Colts. 'If you try one more move like that, I'll drop you where you stand. Get me?'

'You think you're a big man right now, Manders,' gritted the other as he got slowly to his feet, wiping away the blood from his chin with the back of his sleeve, 'but you won't look so big when Wicker has you dangling from the end of a rope. And I'll be there to see it happen. Make no mistake about that.'

'Somehow, I don't think so.' Bret motioned him on to his horse, waited until he had mounted, then swung up into his own saddle. His head and shoulders ached with the blows he had received, and it was still difficult to see clearly. His eyes were painful and watered with the grit still in them.

They rode for the rest of the afternoon, hugging the trail, while the sun gradually lowered itself through the glaring arch of the sky, a sullen red ball that still had a searing heat in it. Not until shortly before nightfall did they come in sight of the Redden spread, cross the river and into the green pasture land. After the blistering heat of the desert, this patch of green was a soothing thing to the eyes, a balm to Bret's spirit. He felt a deep weariness inside him, and he found his fingers gripping the reins a little more tightly than was absolutely necessary.

In front of him, the gunhawk rode in sullen silence, occasionally lifting his hand to rub his battered features or to drink from the water bottle at his side. He had not spoken a single word since they had left the waterhole and Bret knew that he was still trying to devise some means of getting away before they reached the ranch. Once there, he would be as good as dead.

They entered the trees on the upland trail then headed their horses down towards the ranch. A small group of men were already outside the ranch house and they came forward as the two men approached. Redden was with them and he eyed Bret critically. 'You look as if you've been in a fight,' he said slowly. Then his gaze swept over the other man. 'I see you brought him in alive. That's better than I'd hoped. We ought to be able to get plenty out of him if he'll talk.'

Bret gave a quick nod as he slid out of the saddle and handed the horse over to one of the men. 'He'll talk,' he said grimly. 'I think he realizes just where he stands now. Wicker will soon get to hear of this and I wouldn't like to be in his shoes if he comes hunting for him. And I've a hunch that Wicker isn't the kind of man who takes to bunglers very kindly. He'll be thinking up something fitting for your past night's work.'

'If you think you can scare me, you're wrong,' grunted the other as he was hauled out of the saddle. 'Once the sheriff gets to hear of this kidnapping. Once he gets a posse together, he'll soon put this to right.'

'I reckon everyone here knows about Sheriff Veldon,' said Redden quietly, stepping up to the other and looking him squarely in the eye. 'He's a sheep who follows everything that Wicker says. He ain't the law in these parts, any more than you are. Wicker is the only one who gives the orders around here and that's something we aim to stop.'

There was a little of the fear which Bret had seen out on the desert in the man's face as the men closed in on him and herded him towards the house, Redden came over to Bret. 'You did a fine job there,' he said quietly. 'I never figgered you'd get him, least of all alive. Do you reckon he knows much about Wicker's plans?'

'That depends. Ever seen this man before?'

'Sure. His name's Williams. He's the foreman over at the Lazy V ranch.'

'Foreman.' Bret raised his brows slightly. 'That's even better than I had figured. If anybody is in Wicker's confidence, he is. I think he can tell us quite a lot. But we'll have to go about this the right way. We don't have much time, but we mustn't let him know that.'

'I get your meaning.' The other fell into step beside him as they walked back towards the ranch. 'I've sent word to Nolan and he's coming right over. After the defeat Wicker received last night, I doubt whether he'll strike again so soon, but there ought to be plenty of men left to handle him now.'

'Glad to hear it. I've somehow got the feeling that we've under-estimated Wicker. I'll admit that this guy Williams tried his darnedest to kill me last night. If I hadn't spotted him when I did, he would have done it too. But this whole affair has got me worried. It's nothing I can put my finger on definitely. Just a nagging little voice at the back of my mind telling me that there's more trouble ahead of us, big trouble and that pretty soon we'll find ourselves right in the middle of it.' He paused for a moment, drew in a deep breath, then shrugged his shoulders. 'Still, that's enough of my hunches for the moment. What say we go in and see if this *hombre* will talk willingly or whether we'll have to force the truth out of him. I've a feeling that he knows plenty.'

They found Williams seated in a tall, high-backed chair near the fire. He was eyeing the assembled men warily and there was fear in his eyes. Redden went forward and stood in front of the other, his hands near the butts of his Colts.

'So you're Williams, Wicker's foreman,' he said softly, evenly, and there was a threat in the quiet voice. 'I've heard about you. A big man so long as you have a couple of dozen armed men riding at your back, so long as you can go out and plunder the homesteaders, or an unde-fended ranch. But now you aren't so sure of yourself. Now you're all alone and Darby Wicker isn't here to back you up. It ain't a nice feeling, is it?'

'If you're figgering on getting me to talk, then you're wasting your time,' snarled the other savagely. He pulled himself tautly upright in his chair. 'Once Wicker hears about this, he'll finish you once and for all.'

'By the time he gets around to figuring out that some-thing must have happened to you along the desert trail, or even across the border, it'll be too late for him to send out another messenger,' said Bret quietly. 'And I doubt whether he'll worry his head overmuch as to your condition.'

He said quietly to Redden: 'Somehow, I don't think he's going to talk without a little persuasion.'

5

Revelation

After a while, it became obvious that Williams knew little of Wicker's future plans beyond the fact that he intended to get help from south of the border. The Lazy V gang had lost almost half of their number in the two skirmishes with the ranchers and Wicker was determined to remain at the ranch until he received his urgently-needed reinforcements.

Redden looked across at Bret as Williams finished speaking. There was a tight expression on his face. 'It's beginning to look as though we might break this devil if we could only strike now and strike hard.'

Bret rubbed his chin reflectively. 'That's possible,' he admitted slowly, 'but somehow, I've a feeling that it won't be as simple as that.'

'You think this man is lying, that Wicker is setting a trap for us, hoping that we will go in and attack him?' asked Nolan who had just arrived.

Bret said briskly: 'Not exactly. Williams is telling the truth as far as he knows it, but I doubt whether that's all there is to it. Wicker is too cunning a man to leave himself as defenceless as he seems.' There was a dead silence in the room for long moments, a silence broken only by the harsh breathing of the prisoner, lying slumped in the chair, his head lolling forward on to his chest. His eyes were half closed and there was an ugly bruise on his forehead and more fresh blood trickling down his chin.

'What should we do then?' Redden shifted uneasily from one foot to the other. 'Wait until those bandits do arrive from the south? Every day that we delay is working in Wicker's favour. We can't afford to wait too long.'

'I know. Give me twenty-four hours. I'll ride into Sundown tomorrow and do a little scouting around. If what Williams said was true, then there'll be very few of the Lazy V riders in town, apart from Sheriff Veldon and I reckon I can handle him.'

'That makes sense,' agreed Redden. 'Need any of my men to go with you, just in case there is trouble?'

'I'll take half a dozen with me,' nodded Bret. 'That ought to be enough. In the meantime, I could do with some sleep and a bite to eat. Better take care of our prisoner. See that he doesn't escape and warn Wicker of what has happened.'

'Don't worry,' retorted the other grimly. 'I know just the place for him. I can promise you he'll make no further trouble.'

Half an hour later, after finishing an excellent meal, Bret went up to his room and was asleep within minutes. Not even the dull ache which suffused the whole of his body could keep him awake. He woke to someone shaking him by the shoulder and opened his eyes to see Redden standing beside the bed. Sunlight was streaming in through the open windows.

'I didn't want to wake you so early,' said the other quietly, 'but if you're to make it into town, I reckon you'd better get started in an hour or so.'

'Sure. Thanks.' Bret swung his legs to the floor. He washed, shaved and combed his hair, put on a clean shirt to replace that which had become stained and sand-smeared the previous day. When he went down into the kitchen half an hour later, he felt fit and refreshed. Breakfast was ready for him and he sat down with Redden and Nolan. He was mildly surprised to find that he was still ravenously hungry even after the meal he had eaten late the previous night.

'I've warned the men to be ready to ride with you, Bret,' said Redden quietly, glancing up. 'They're eager for a fight and I don't think you'll have much trouble even if you do run into any of the gunhawks from the Lazy V.'

'I'm not anticipating trouble,' said Bret calmly. 'But if it comes, I know how to meet it. I think I'll pay a call on the sheriff when I get there. One or two things I want to know.'

'Think he'll talk?' Nolan leaned forward in his chair, resting his weight on his elbows. 'He's in this up to his neck.'

'Sure, I realize that. But he's also a scared little man. He values his hide far more than anything else in this world. If he once gets it into his head that Wicker is going to lose out on this particular deal, he'll spill everything he knows. The trouble is that even after his last two defeats, and with only half of his fighting force still alive, Wicker is still a big man in Sundown.' He smacked the fist of one hand into the palm of the other with a gesture of exasperation. 'If only the homesteaders and the rest of the smaller ranchers would see things as you do, then we would have a fighting force ready to meet anything; even those killers he sent for from Mexico.'

'At least, we stopped that little plan,' said Redden in a relieved tone. 'I hate to think of what would have happened if he had succeeded in getting word through to that bandit chief, Gonzales. He's one of the most vicious killers this side of the Rio Grande. He'll stop at nothing; and unlike Wicker, he doesn't kill for gain, for power. He kills for the sheer delight of it. The same goes for his men. To be quite honest, I'd sooner face a horde of Apaches on the warpath than Gonzales and his gang.'

'I hope that it never comes to that showdown then,' said Bret fervently. But in spite of the conviction in his voice, there was that nagging little devil at the back of his mind with its soundless warning.

Half an hour later, they hit the trail and headed for Sundown. Here, among the trees and the stretching green of the pasture, there was none of that flaming, blistering heat which Bret had endured the previous two days. The air had a crisp, fresh quality, went down into his lungs like wine. This would be a beautiful country, he reflected, if only it were cleared of men like Wicker. Sooner or later, more of the homesteaders would move in from the east, would come to build up a new and virile nation, would bring with them the ways of a sturdy and independent people. The frontier would expand westwards until it reached the shores of the mighty Pacific itself. And even then, the march of progress would not be halted. The railroad would come west with the pioneers. The roads would be built, new towns and cities would spring up in the places where there was now nothing but sage brush and wilderness.

He could see it all in his mind's eye as he rode with the small bunch of stern and tight-lipped men. But there were a lot of difficulties to be overcome. There were many more men like Darby Wicker who cared for nothing but themselves, who wanted the power and the glory, who went about getting it by murder and any other unscrupulous means and who retarded progress by many years.

'There's a bunch of riders over there, moving fast,' said one of the men, pointing.

Bret lifted his head, cursed himself for day-dreaming at a time such as this, saw the cloud of dust in the distance and could just make out the shapes of several horsemen moving along the higher trail which ran almost parallel to that along which they were travelling.

'Anybody make out who they are?' he snapped briskly. 'They seem to be heading for town.'

'Doesn't look like any of the Lazy V riders to me,' grunted another man thickly. 'They don't seem to have spotted us. If they're from the Lazy V, they may try to make a fight of it before we reach Sundown.'

'Keep your eyes open from now on.' Bret spurred his mount forward. 'We don't want to run into an ambush.'

They rode into Sundown two hours later. There was no sign of the bunch of riders they had seen on the trail although there were several horses hitched outside the Golden Ace saloon. Bret eyed them with a keen glance as he slid from the saddle outside the sheriff's office. They did not carry the brand of the Lazy V and he guessed that they were men from one of the other ranches in the surrounding territory. He felt a little more at ease, but still wary as he stepped up on the boardwalk and pushed open the door to the sheriff's office.

The room beyond was empty but a moment later, there was the sound of footsteps coming along the narrow passage which led to the cells at the rear of the building and Veldon appeared in the doorway at the far side of the room. He did not see Bret immediately and had his back to him as he replaced one of the keys on a hook on the wall. Then he turned, saw the other and his jaw sagged open in surprise.

'Manders,' he said thickly. His eyes lifted to the men who stood at Bret's back and there was a little twinge of fear on his face as he recognized them. 'Just what is the meaning of this? Why come riding into town with these armed men at your back? Looking for trouble?'

'Not exactly,' said Bret easily. 'Just being prepared for it this time. I gathered the last time I was here that my presence wasn't exactly welcome. I hope that your attitude has changed a little since then.'

'My attitude has always been that anyone is allowed in Sundown provided that they haven't broken the law,' said the other stiffly. He seemed to have got a little of his courage back as he walked forward and seated himself in the chair behind the desk. He leaned forward, so that the flap of his jacket fell open deliberately, showing the star pinned to his shirt. Bret had the feeling that he had done this for a purpose, hoping to prevent any trouble, especially on the part of the other men, by showing them that they were dealing with the law.

Grinning mirthlessly, Bret walked forward until he leaned forward over the desk, towering over the portly figure of the sheriff. 'I don't aim to start trouble, Sheriff,' he said ominously, 'but if there is any, then I do aim to finish it. Get that straight from the beginning and you and I will get along fine.'

'Just what is it that you want with me?' asked the other, cringing back in the chair a little way. 'If you've come about Darby Wicker, then I'm afraid that this is completely out of my hands.'

'You heard that he tried to attack both the Redden ranch and that belonging to Nolan,' said Bret with a hard edge to his voice. 'We've also got proof that he's been systematically rustling cattle from every ranch in the territory, changing brands. We can also lay several murders on him; but you still say that this doesn't interest you.'

'I said that it was out of my hands,' retorted the other. Beads of sweat had popped out on his fleshy forehead and were running in streaks down his cheeks. He pulled out his handkerchief and mopped his face with it, although the room was far from warm. 'Wicker has holed himself up in his ranch outside the town and —'

'You claiming that this is outside your jurisdiction,' growled one of the men behind Bret. He stepped forward, gun sliding from its holster, 'because if you are —'

'Steady,' said Bret. 'Whatever happens we don't want to be charged with the murder of the sheriff.'

'That's better,' said Veldon, getting to his feet. 'If you kill me, you'll be hunted for the rest of your lives.' He swallowed thickly, then went on in a low tone. 'I know what Wicker is. He's a cold-blooded murderer and a cattle thief.

He's been stringing this town along ever since he arrived here eight years ago.'

'Then why haven't you done something about it?' demanded Bret harshly. 'The decent people here outnumber those gunslingers at the Lazy V by almost a hundred to one.'

Veldon's lips twisted into a cynical grin. 'That's perfectly true. But you just go out there and try to get together a posse to go hunt him down. I tried all day yesterday and this morning too. Not one man would volunteer to be deputized.'

Bret doubted whether this was the complete truth, but he could quite see the other's point of view. The townsfolk would not rise against Wicker so long as he had those gunmen at his ranch. Also, it was highly likely that he had some of his men to spread the word that Gonzales and his gang were heading north to help him defeat the ranchers. Even the thought of this would be sufficient to keep the people of Sundown in check.

'They're all afraid of the Mexican bandits that Wicker tried to send for. Is that it?' Bret watched the little sheriff closely, trying to analyse the different expressions which flickered across his features.

'I'm afraid I don't quite understand,' he said hesitantly. 'The word was that he has already sent for them.' He paused, moistened his lips. 'But how do you know this? It was supposed to be a secret.'

'We know it,' said Bret quietly, 'because we have got his foreman prisoner at the Redden place. He never made it to the border. That's one of Wicker's plans which has failed.'

'So you were watching the desert trail.' The other seemed to be speaking his thoughts out aloud. 'I might have guessed. But the important point is, does Wicker know this?'

'I doubt it. But he will in a few days' time when no help comes from south of the border. Then he'll either have to make one last all-out bid to defeat us, or move out of the territory.'

'He will never leave like that,' said the other with conviction. 'Sometimes I think that more than anything else, it is pride which drives him to do these things.'

'Pride.' Bret spoke with a bitter savagery. 'Pride! Sheriff, I know this man Wicker of old. I know who he is and what he is. And believe me, pride does not enter into it. I remember him when he fought in the war.'

The other looked surprised at this sudden outburst. 'You knew him during the war. I understood that he fought for the South.'

'He fought with Quantrill and his band of renegades.' Bret spoke through thinned lips. 'He murdered innocent men and women. He was there when they captured Lawrence and put it to the fire and sword. That wasn't war, but an inhuman massacre worse than anything perpetrated by the Indians. At least they were known to be savages, but Quantrill and men like Wicker were supposed to be human beings.'

'So that's why you've been hounding him all these years.' There was a new respect in the sheriff's voice and a touch of something which could have been awe. 'I might have guessed it was something like that. It must have been something personal to make you hate him so much.'

'He was directly responsible for the murder of my parents, for the whole of my family. They never had a chance, I swore then that I'd follow him no matter where he tried to hide and that I'd be the one to kill him. He knows this too. That's why he's so determined that I've got to die. The only fear I've ever had during the whole of these past eight years, the only nightmare that ever haunted my dreams, was that I might run him to earth only to find that somebody else had killed him before me. But thank God, he's still alive. He can still suffer for a little while longer before the end comes.'

'You seem all-fired certain that you're going to kill

him,' muttered the sheriff. Now that the hatred and anger had been transferred from him to Wicker, he was no longer so afraid.

'I'll kill him. This has been eating at me for too long for it to be thwarted now.' He turned to the men behind him. 'Two of you remain here and keep an eye on him. Not that I think he might try to get word to Wicker, but just to be on the safe side.'

'Don't worry,' nodded one of the men, a tall, husky cowpoke with flaming red hair and a long, thoughtful face. 'We'll see that he doesn't cause any trouble.'

Bret nodded. 'The rest of you come with me. There are a few questions I need answering and I know just the person to give us those answers.'

The sheriff looked up at him. He said just a trifle quickly: 'You won't get anyone in Sundown to help you, Manders. They're all too scared of Wicker for that.'

'Not all of them,' said Bret, relishing the look of amazement on the other's face. 'There are still one or two citizens who aren't afraid of Wicker and what he stands for.'

Veldon nodded. 'Wicker was wondering how you managed to get your information about the Nolan raid. He guessed it had to be someone here in town.'

Bret nodded swiftly, then stepped out into the street, throwing a swift glance in both directions. In the late morning sunlight, it looked peaceful and normal. A horse champed at its bit outside the saloon. The sound of music came from the saloon. This was how it could be all the time, if they could remove the menace of Darby Wicker and his gunslingers, thought Bret inwardly as he led the way to the saloon. Pushing open the batwing doors he stepped inside, eyes taking in everything at a single glance. The guy behind the piano glanced up in surprise, stopped playing. The barman at the back of the long counter stared at him as if were seeing a ghost.

'Just keep playing,' said Bret calmly, nodding towards

the piano player. 'There's ain't no call for alarm. We're just here on a friendly visit.'

The man turned back to the piano and began playing again, but it was clear that his heart was no longer in it. Men like these could mean only one thing – trouble.

Bret walked up to the bar and spoke softly to the man behind it: 'Where can I find Fay Saunders?'

The other's eyes narrowed and for a moment it looked as if he did not intend to give any answer, then he licked his lips drily and said, equally softly: 'She's upstairs. Shall I tell her you're here?'

'No need to put yourself out.' Bret nodded towards the men at the bar. 'Just give my friends a drink. I'll find her myself.'

He made his way quickly up the stairway, reached a long corridor at the top and paused to find his bearings. He had entered this place from the rear the last time and everything seemed strange. Finally, however, he found the room and rapped sharply on the door. There was silence for a moment, then he heard the rustle of a gown at the other side of the door and Fay's voice called: 'Yes, who is it?'

'Bret Manders,' he said softly.

The door opened a moment later and she stood on one side to let him in, glancing quickly along the corridor before closing the door behind him. 'Are you all alone?' she asked quickly.

He shook his head. 'I brought a few men from the Redden ranch with me this time. Purely as a precaution, although I doubt if Wicker will try anything.'

'You must have killed a lot of his men,' she said, with a faint smile playing on her red lips. 'He was in a terrible rage when he rode into town yesterday.'

She sank down on to the low couch and motioned him to sit beside her. 'But what about that Mexican friend of his — Gonzales. You know, of course, that he's sent word to him. That he'll come riding north as fast as he can collect his men together. And when that happens, you'll stand very little chance at all unless you can get the Army to act.'

Bret smiled. 'There's very little to be afraid of, really,' he said easily. 'We guessed that he'd try to get help from the south. I watched the desert trail and picked up his foreman as he was riding to fetch Gonzales. We've got him over at the Redden ranch this very minute. He told us as much as he knew, after we had persuaded him a little. But unfortunately all he did know was that he had been ordered to warn Gonzales and fetch him running. I thought you might be able to fill in a few of the missing details for us.'

'Williams!' There was a look of puzzlement and something else in the girl's eyes. 'You mean that you only caught him?'

Bret felt a cold stab at his brain. The little germ was beginning to yell at him at the back of his mind, more strongly now. Was there something he had overlooked? Had he been too confident in expecting Wicker to send only one man? The girl's next words confirmed this.

'But he sent two more men, Bret. They left almost immediately after Williams and they were riding to the south, keeping away from the recognized trails. One of the men from the Lazy V came in yesterday and got a little drunk. It wasn't too difficult to get the information out of him.'

'I see.' Bret tightened his lips into a thin, hard line across the centre of his rugged features. He nodded his head numbly. This was what he had been afraid of all along, ever since he had captured Williams. This was what that little voice had been trying to tell him. It was far too late now to send any men after those two gunhawks. They would have two days' start by now and moving directly across country they could be over the Mexican frontier.

'What are you going to do now, Bret?' She looked at him closely. 'You can't stop them from getting word to Gonzales. He'll be here within four, maybe five, days. And when he does come, he'll bring a hundred or so killers with him. You won't stand a chance against them.'

Bret rose swiftly to his feet and began pacing the room, his hands clasped behind his back, his brow puckered in worried concentration. An icy little chill was shivering along his spine as he realized the full enormity of the situation. Inwardly, he cursed himself for not having recognized this possibility before. Wicker must be laughing now, he thought angrily, laughing at the easy way in which he had tricked him.

But the anger did not last long. Bret had come through too much during the past ten years, first in the war and then in his wanderings over the western frontier searching for Wicker, to allow himself to be panicked into rash decisions and foolish ideas. There had to be something they could do to face this attack when it came. His first thought was to ride as fast as he could for Fort Laramie, put his case to the commander there and ask for troops, but he recognized immediately that he could expect little help from that source. There were too few troops available to patrol the hundreds of miles of frontier.

Fay watched him seriously. 'All of these people are going to lose their homes, their ranches, everything, unless we can do something,' she said soberly. 'Wicker won't forget what has happened and once he has these men behind him, his vengeance will be swift and terrible. Believe me, I know this man, Bret. He's a fiend from hell itself.'

'I've had dealings with him myself in the past,' grated the other. He paused by the window. 'If only we could rouse the people in the town, get them to band together and fight, we could destroy him before these bandits get here. But they won't listen.'

'They're afraid,' she said softly. 'They see what has happened before to any others who dared to stand up to Darby Wicker. So far, he's made no move towards them and they believe that so long as they remain strictly neutral

in this matter, things will always remain like that. You'll
stand very little chance of convincing them otherwise.'

'That's what I was afraid of.' His hands clenched and
unclenched spasmodically by his sides. 'Even though
we've shown that Wicker and his hired killers can be
beaten at their own game, they'll never listen to me.' He
stared hard at the girl.

'Fay, you've lived here almost all of your life. These
people know you. They trust you. Would they listen to you
if you pleaded with them?'

She looked at him in silence for a long moment, then
pursed her lips. 'They might, but I doubt it. I'm not very
popular with most of them, simply because they think I'm
in with Wicker.'

'Do your best,' he urged. 'In the meantime, I'll ride
around and talk with the other ranchers. They may listen.
If they do, we'll work out some kind of plan. Whatever we
decide, we'll have to move fast. Another five days at the
latest and all hell is due to erupt in Sundown.'

That afternoon, he rode to one of the smaller ranches
some five miles out of Sundown. It stood in a pleasant
valley and as he rode through the boundary wire, he
wondered why Wicker hadn't cast envious eyes on it
earlier. Perhaps, he reflected, the other had been intent
on snapping up the bigger places first, leaving these lesser
ranches until he had built up an unassailable position for
himself. As he rode along, he noticed several small herds
of prime beef cattle in the grazing land, a few cowhands
keeping a close watch on them.

He reached the corral in front of the house, then
reined his horse as a harsh voice said: 'That's far enough,
mister. Just keep your hands where I can see 'em and slide
down off that saddle, easy like. No tricks mind.'

Bret complied, noticing the three rifles which were
trained on him. One of the men rose up from behind the
low wall in front of the corral and came forward, not
taking his eyes off Bret.

'What you doing on this land?' he enquired. 'Don't you know that it's private property?' The barrel of the rifle never wavered, fixed on his chest.

'I came to see the owner of the ranch,' he said quietly, keeping his hands in the open, away from the guns at his hips. It was more than likely that he could outshoot these three men if he tried, even though they had the drop on him, but he recognized that there was no danger of them opening fire, that they merely had orders to keep out strangers, or take them to the Boss.

The man's brows lifted into an interrogatory line. 'What you want to see him for, mister? You don't look like one of those hired killers from the Lazy V place, but here we take no chances.'

Bret smiled. Out of the corner of his eye, he noticed the other two men moving forward, one on either side of him. They couldn't be more than eighteen years old, either of them, he thought inwardly, little more than boys. But there was a fierce glitter to their eyes which told him that they would stand no nonsense, that they would shoot him if they had to.

'Do I get to see the owner?' he asked lightly. 'It's important.'

The man in front of him hesitated, then said sharply. 'Throw down those guns of yours and then step forward slowly. Don't try to pull them on me. You'll be a dead man if you do.'

Very gently, Bret eased the Colts from their holsters and let them drop on to the ground at his feet. One of the boys came forward at a signal from the other man and kicked them away without lowering his rifle.

'See if he has any more hidden away on him,' said the other briskly.

Bret waited until the boy run his hand over him, then stepped back satisfied. 'He's clean, Pa,' he said quietly.

'Fair enough.' The other motioned with his rifle. 'Just move ahead of me, mister, to the ranch house. Then we'll listen to what you've got to say.'

The room into which he was shown was small and sparsely furnished, but there was an air about the room which suggested that it had been lived in for a long time. There was a low desk in the corner, close to the open window and behind it sat a tall, grey-haired man whom Bret guessed to be in his late fifties. The other looked up in surprise as he was pushed into the room.

'We stopped this *hombre* as he was riding through the pasture, Boss,' said the other man. 'He was armed but he made no resistance when we stopped him. He says he wants to speak to you.'

The grey-haired man pushed back his chair and regarded Bret with a long, cool stare. Then he said courteously. 'It isn't often that we have visitors here. My name is Reed, Adam Reed. I own this spread. It isn't large, but for an old man like me, it's enough.'

Bret nodded and seated himself into the chair which the other indicated. 'My name is Bret Manders,' he said softly. 'You won't know me, I'm afraid. I arrived here only a few days ago and —'

The other smiled broadly. 'On the contrary I do know you, Mr Manders. Who hasn't heard of you in this territory? The man who sent Darby Wicker running back to the Lazy V ranch with his tail between his legs like a whipped dog. No one could possibly do a thing like that without being known. Your fame has gone before you, whether you like it or not.'

'Then if you know so much about me, you can probably guess why I'm here.'

The other placed the tips of his fingers together, leaning on his elbows. 'I'm afraid not,' he said calmly. 'Unless you come to warn me that my ranch is the next to be attacked by Wicker.'

Bret shook his head. 'Not exactly, I've reason to believe that Wicker will remain where he is for the next few days until he gets help from Mexico.'

'Brigands, you mean?' queried the other. There was not the slightest change in the expression on his face to give an indication as to the thoughts which were passing through his mind at that moment.

'You could call them that, if you wished,' agreed Bret. 'But I would simply call them murderers. Professional killers. They murder innocent men and women simply for the sheer pleasure of it. They're far worse than the Indians and God knows they're bad enough'

'But what has all this got to do with me – or my ranch?' There was a faint look of puzzlement on the other's face as he leaned back in his chair.

'Don't you realise the danger you're in?' said Bret earnestly. 'Can't you see it? Or are you so blind that you let it go unnoticed until it's too late.'

'I'm afraid I don't quite understand you, Mr Manders. To the best of my knowledge no one has yet made any threats towards me. Are you suggesting that I am in danger from Wicker? But that is ridiculous. My spread is so small, scarcely three hundred head of cattle. This is just chickenfeed as far as he is concerned. No – I understand Mr Wicker. He is after far bigger things than my ranch.'

'Darby Wicker is after everything he can lay his hands on,' Bret spoke quickly and earnestly. 'He won't rest until he owns everything in this area. Why do you think he's trying to run the homesteaders off their property, getting the bank in Sundown, which he controls, to foreclose on their mortgages, and buying up their land at a fraction of its proper price? He wants everything which lies between the desert and the mountains to the west. Unless we attack him now, we'll never stop him. Surely you must see that?'

'Mr Manders,' said the other patiently. 'All that matters to me at the moment is that people leave me to manage my own affairs. I must admit that in the past, I have met Wicker only once. Besides, what can I do to help you? I have five men on my ranch apart from three I need to watch the herd. You've met most of them already. An old man of almost sixty and two young boys just turned eighteen. Are you seriously asking that I should send them out, turn them over to you so that you can put them into a fight with brigands from over the border. No, Mr Manders, I'm afraid that's out of the question.' He smiled broadly, shook his head. 'I think I can handle Wicker my own way and that won't be with violence. As for the other ranchers, well, of course they can do as they wish, but if I were asked, I'm afraid that my advice to them would be to keep out of this range war that seems to be blowing up in this corner of the territory. No good can come of it for anyone.'

'Then you refuse your help to us?' Bret rose to his feet, trying hard to control the anger in his voice.

'Please don't misinterpret my words,' said the other smoothly. 'I cannot help you. Even if I wished to do so, with the small number of men I have on the ranch, it would be foolish of me to send any of them to help you in what must surely be a futile effort on your part.'

'I see.' Bret gave a quick nod of his head, hitched his gunbelt a little higher. 'Then there seems to be nothing more to be said. It's a little unfortunate that a lot of good men, a host of innocent women and children are going to have to die, simply because of men like you. The West wasn't won by faint-hearted men who allowed life to rule them. And we won't keep this heritage of ours very long if we're content to sit back and let men like Darby Wicker step in and wrest it from us.'

'I'm sorry.' The other spread his hands in a non-committal gesture. 'I only wish there was something I could do. But as it is —'

'I know,' muttered Bret shortly. 'You'll sit here until one morning you'll wake up to find that Darby Wicker has stepped in and taken over your ranch. Then you'll squeal for help, but by that time it'll be far too late.'

Turning quickly on his heel he walked out of the house to where his mount stood tethered to the rail. The old man came forward with his guns and handed them over to him. There was a perplexed look on his face. He said softly: 'I heard you say that your name was Bret Manders.' He waited until Bret had swung himself up into the saddle. 'I know it ain't none of my business, but you'll get none of the smaller ranchers to help you. You'll only be wasting your time trying to get them to throw in with you. They're scared of Wicker and in spite of what you've done in the past, they still aren't convinced that you can beat him with the few men you've got.'

Bret nodded with tightened lips, sliding the Colts into the holsters. 'I reckon you're right,' he sighed. 'The big trouble is that if they hesitate for another few days, nothing is going to help them.'

The old man nodded. 'Yeah. I heard about Wicker sending for the Mexicans. I recall the time when they last came over the border. Three, mebbe four years ago, plundering and murderin'. I guess most of the folk who were around here at that time have long memories and they're afraid the same thing will happen again.'

'Was it bad?'

'Pretty bad. They had to bring out the military from Fort Laramie. There were more troops stationed there in those days and they managed to drive Gonzales and his half-breeds back clear across the border.'

'If they're hoping for that to happen again this time, they're in for a shock. There aren't enough troops at Fort Laramie for any to be sent here. Gonzales and his men will have little or no opposition this time.'

He wheeled his mount and rode out of the ranch, reaching the trail half an hour later. Visits to two other ranches soon confirmed what he had already guessed. There would be no help forthcoming from this source. The ranch owners listened to his arguments, then shrugged their shoulders and maintained that there was nothing they could do to help, that they needed all of the men they had on their payrolls to work on the ranch.

He reached the Redden ranch in a tired and dispirited mood. As he swung out of the saddle, Redden came out of the ranch house and walked over to him.

'You don't look as though you've had much success with the other ranchers,' he said quietly.

Bret shook his head. 'They listened, but that was all. Everyone seemed to think that they had nothing to fear from Wicker so long as they took no part in this. They're like a host of ostriches, burying their heads in the sand. They either can't see that he'll turn on them as soon as he's finished with us, or they don't want to see. It makes little difference. They won't help us. We can't count on them, I'm afraid.'

'I suspected as much from the beginning. But we had to try. We'll have to make other plans.'

'Other plans,' said Bret bitterly. 'What other plans can we make? With only thirty or so men against a hundred and more, the odds aren't loaded in our favour. And if we strike now, we don't stand much of a chance, not so long as he's barricaded behind his own walls.'

'Dynamite,' suggested the other. 'We used it once before with some success. It might be possible for some of us to sneak up on them during the night and use the dynamite to breach the walls of their ranch.'

Bret pondered that for a moment, then shook his head. 'Far too risky,' he said finally. 'They'll have guards posted along the trail to the Lazy V and traps set close to the ranch house. Besides, I don't want to run the risk of losing more men. If we failed, and I'm quite certain that we must fail in that scheme, it means we'll have very few men left to pull a trigger.'

'So we wait for them to come and fight it out with them? Is that it?'

Bret sighed. It was difficult to answer the other's question. The refusal of the smaller ranchers to help him had been a severe blow to any plans he had in mind. Without their aid, he would be forced to think again. 'There is one thing that we must do,' he said, turning. 'Have you a man with a fast horse?'

'Of course. Three if you wish.' The other regarded him for a moment in surprise at the sudden question.

'One ought to be enough. I'll need someone to watch the trail, to give us advance warning of their approach. If we know how many men he has with him, at least we'll know what we're up against.'

'I'll send one of the men off this very day,' promised the other. 'You're expecting them in four or five days' time?'

Bret nodded. His face was lined and furrowed with strain. He knew only too well that when the combined forces of Wicker and Gonzales struck, Sundown would be taken in a couple of bloody, terrible days. It would be Lawrence all over again, with the same senseless murders of women and children, the burning down of the tall buildings. He shivered as the scene impressed itself upon his mind's eye.

As the days passed and there was no further move on Wicker's part, it became obvious that he was playing a waiting game. Whether or not he was aware that this foreman had been captured and was Bret's prisoner, it was impossible to tell. The rider had been sent out to watch the trail for the approach of Gonzales and his men and in the meantime, feverish preparations were taking place at the Redden ranch. At Bret's suggestion, they had agreed to pool their resources, and Nolan had realized that if they split their forces, it would be relatively easy for them to be overwhelmed and that the only chance they had would be to amalgamate and defend one of the ranches.

Bret knew what a decision it must have been for Nolan, to bring his men away from his own ranch so that they might defend Redden's. Virtually, it meant leaving his own spread at the mercy of Wicker and the Mexicans if they decided to attack there first. He did not doubt that Wicker had his spies out, watching the range, and would know by now of what was happening. Barricades were erected around the ranch house and anything inflammable was taken from the barns which could not be easily defended. This time, they wanted no chance of fire being used to drive them out into the open and on to the guns of the brigands.

Fortunately, they had plenty of ammunition and also a further supply of dynamite which was used to mine the trails approaching the Redden ranch. It was going to be imperative for them to kill as many men as possible before they got to the ranch.

Three days later, as Bret stepped out onto the broad veranda of the ranch house, he spotted the rider coming up fast in the distance. One glance was sufficient to tell him that this was the man that Redden had sent to watch the trail. He called Redden and the two of them went out into the courtyard and waited while the other rode up to them. The man slipped out of the saddle and ran forward. He was breathing heavily and had clearly been riding the stallion to the limit in his attempt to keep ahead of the approaching men.

'Well?' said Redden tightly. 'What is it? What's the news?'

'They're on their way,' gasped the other hoarsely. He jerked the words out like pistol shots. 'I spotted them about fifteen or twenty miles back to the south-east. They didn't seem to be hurrying none like you suggested, Bret. But there are sure plenty of them. I counted about a hundred, possibly more moving up behind, but I couldn't be sure of that.'

'But you are sure that these are Gonzales's men? There's no doubt about that?'

The other nodded quickly. 'I saw Gonzales with my own eyes. I would never forget that man, not if I lived to be a hundred.'

'So. Now we know.' In spite of the seriousness of the situation, Bret felt a sudden uplifting of the spirit, a warm pulsing glow inside him. Now they knew exactly what it was they had to face. Possibly thirty men from the Lazy V and about a hundred or so riding up with Gonzales. A hundred and fifty men against thirty at the most. He grimaced. On the face of it, they stood no chance at all. He knew now why the smaller ranches had refused to throw in their lot with him.

'How long before they get here?' he asked the man quickly.

'Two days. Not longer.' There was a little trace of excitement in the man's voice which Bret did not fail to notice. 'I spotted the two men whom Wicker sent riding with them. By now Gonzales will know everything that has happened here. Perhaps that is why he has brought so many men. It looks as though he's bringing his whole force.'

'We'll have to delay them as much as we can,' said Bret decisively. 'Engage them on the very edge of the spread and fight for every inch of the ground, pulling back to the ranch itself only when we're forced to do so by sheer weight of numbers or to prevent ourselves from being surrounded and cut off from the others. That way, at least we stand a chance.'

'There were only a few of them carrying rifles,' said the man as they went into the house. 'Most of them just had revolvers.'

'That means nothing,' declared Redden. 'Wicker will have plenty of rifles. He can supply every man with one.' He pursed his lips into a thin line. 'Two days. And we can say that they'll spend at least one night at the Lazy V ranch while Wicker explains what he wants them to do. Whether they attack Sundown, or come straight here in the hope of finishing us off quickly, will depend upon him. My guess, for what it's worth, is that they'll come here first.'

'I agree with that,' nodded Bret. 'Sundown is of little danger to them now. But they have to destroy us.' He glanced at Redden. 'Does every man know what he has to do? When they attack, there won't be time for explanations."

'They're all ready.' Redden looked out across the rolling pastures which stretched in every direction as far as the eye could see; and Bret knew what thoughts were passing through his mind at that particular moment. He was visualizing this place as it would be if Gonzales and his men overran it. It had taken many years for the other to build it up like this and now there was the distinct possibility that everything he held dear would be battered down and destroyed. Bret threw a quick glance in the direction of Nolan, talking to a small group of cowpokes. For him, it would be even worse, knowing that the chances were high of his spread being destroyed and he not there to raise a hand to prevent it.

It was a damnable pity that the rest of the ranchers were not made of the same stuff as Nolan. These men were the true pioneers of the West, the men who had pushed back the frontier, wrested the land from the Indians, tamed it, ploughed it and set their cattle to graze on its rich green pastures. These were the kind of men who would build the future; not men like Wicker. They were but a phase in the history of the land.

That night, with the slender crescent moon rising over the distant pines, Bret walked around the defences of the spread with Nolan and Redden. Both of the men were oddly silent, obviously engrossed in their own thoughts. As they made their way around the network of barricades which had been set up on either side of the trail, Bret Manders was acutely conscious of the rising tension which was apparent everywhere. In all, they had thirty-one fit men in their force, men who could handle a rifle and would fight well. But the enemy's force outnumbered them by at least six to to one.

Whatever the men lacked, it was certainly not courage; but courage was not enough in this case. The odds were stacked so heavily against them that even the most optimistic did not believe that they would come out on top once the attack was launched.

6

Range War

'Any idea what Gonzales might have in his mind?' asked Bret. He stood on the long veranda outside the Redden ranch, staring moodily into the darkness. It was almost night and a deep, expectant hush seemed to have fallen over everything, enveloping the entire countryside as if beneath a blanket of silence.

'None.' Redden turned slowly. 'He's a damned mean critter. You can't possibly get into his mind to figger out what he's likely to do. With Wicker you do at least know where you stand. His actions are predictable so long as you know what kind of force it is that's driving him. But Gonzales —' He made a slight gesture with his hands. 'He's likely to tie up with Wicker as soon as he gets here, and then ride against us.' The other tightened his lips. 'What's worrying me is that he might insist on taking Sundown first. Wicker needs those men desperately and I reckon he might be forced to agree with Gonzales on that point. If he does, then God help those poor devils in the town.'

'That may be the answer, or part of it. How far to the nearest point where we could attack Gonzales by night?'

The other looked up at him in sharp surprise. 'You're not thinking of fighting him in the open, are you. Bret?

That would be sheer suicide, I thought you'd agreed that we wouldn't split our forces.'

Bret curled his lips back in a fierce grin. 'Gonzales must be pretty sure of himself by now. He'll have been told that the army over at Fort Laramie don't have the men available to stop him this time and he has nothing to fear from them. So I figure that he won't be too careful about posting guards at night.'

'So? Even granting you that much, you wouldn't stand a chance of routing over a hundred men.'

'No.' Bret's voice was cold and decisive, as brittle as ice. 'But we could make certain that he does trail after us, rather than push on into Sundown. Gonzales is a killer, we're all agreed on that point, and he'll think like a killer and not like a tactician. He'll attack blindly against anyone who shoots him up, like a steer being irritated by a bluefly. We'll play the part of the fly, we'll nettle him, lead him away from the trail and on to the southern end of your spread. The rest of the men will be waiting there. Once we have him committed to finishing us, Sundown will be safe for the time being.'

Redden laughed shortly, an ugly sound in the clinging stillness. 'Somehow, at this very moment, I'm not feeling too kindly disposed towards the men and women in Sundown. Seems to me that we're out here risking our ranches, even our precious skins, everything that we own, just to save their miserable lives.'

'I know. Sooner or later they're going to come to their senses. They'll figure out Wicker and Gonzales for what they really are and then they'll take the law out of the hands of puppets like Veldon and into their own.'

'But will any of us be around to see it?'

'Sure. We'll be around.' He tried to force conviction into his deep voice. 'Now, you know the territory around these parts better than most. How will Gonzales ride if he wants to get into Sundown fast?'

'That's easy. He'll take the desert trail as far as Big

Bluffs and then head north through the gulch about five miles south of my spread. Tonight, I'd guess that he's camping out in the desert near one of the waterholes.'

'Good. And tomorrow night?' Bret's tone held a tight edge.

'Not far from the gulch. They'll probably wait to launch their attack in broad daylight; with as many men as that they won't need to strike by night. Besides, Gonzales is a very vain man. He likes his victims to know their destroyer before they die.'

Bret rubbed the side of his face thoughtfully. 'Perhaps that vanity of his will prove to be his downfall. They won't be anticipating trouble of any kind out there at the gulch and if we can get close enough to stampede their horses it should hold them up for a little while and give us more breathing space.' He knew that all it would really do would be to postpone the inevitable, but he deliberately refrained from saying so.

'Could be.' The other nodded his head eagerly. 'How many men were you figgering on taking with you?'

'About a dozen. As I see it, we could be there before dark tomorrow. It's a pretty desolate type of country out there and we could lie up under cover.'

'If this doesn't work we'll never get out of there alive. You know that, I guess. It could turn out to be a trap for us.'

'We'll have to take that chance. We don't want to have to go on to the defensive until we're absolutely forced to do so.'

Swinging north of the pine belt which clustered along the edge of the Redden range, Bret led the others over the hill, hitting the trail which ran through a green grass belt towards the southern side of the ranch. The sun was still high in the heavens and there were still two or three hours of daylight left. Bret had deliberately travelled early, making a wide detour so as to ride the higher trail. By making the detour, he intended to come upon the gulch from a direction which anyone camped there would be the least likely to watch.

Presently, they left the straggling pine belt behind and rode on into more mountainous country, the land broken here and there by flat patches of scrub and ragged sage brush. A few cottonwoods dotted the sides of the trail and here and there they came across patches of more luxuriant growth.

Half an hour later, they reached a series of high, boulder-strewn slopes where the trail narrowed and ran through tall aspens, their leaves gleaming red and gold in the light of the lowering sun. Bret reined in at a point where the trail suddenly widened and waited for the others to come abreast of him.

Redden joined him and stared down through the trees. The sunlight threw long shadows over the trail and much of the underbrush already lay in the darkness. Redden pointed and said: 'They'll come from that direction if our calculations are right. No sign of them yet though.'

Bret threw a swift, calculating glance at the sun, glinting redly through the trees. 'Another hour before nightfall,' he guessed aloud. 'There's plenty of time for them to reach the gulch before then. How much further is it?'

'Another mile or so along the trail,' answered the other. 'We should reach it in about twenty minutes.'

'We'll give the boys a rest here, and then move on.' Bret swung down from the saddle and stretched his aching limbs. They had been riding now for the best part of six hours since leaving the ranch and he recognized that they would need their mounts to be as fresh as possible when they attacked. If they did not succeed in stampeding the bandits' horses, they would have to light out of that gulch in a hurry and every minute would be precious.

Walking to the edge of the trail, Bret stood for a long moment, amid the hushed solitude of the trees looking out over the rolling country which lay spread out beneath him like a multicoloured carpet. The view was breathtaking, magnificent. Down below, perhaps two hundred feet beneath him, the valley stretched away almost unbroken, in three directions. To the south, it reached the edge of the yellow desert which in turn stretched away until it hazed almost imperceptibly with the distant sierras. To the west, where the sun was just beginning to touch the horizon, lay the rich grazing lands of Redden's spread; green and peaceful. But even that was only a surface illusion.

Down in that direction, armed men were camped ready to back him up once he and the others came riding back, luring the Mexican bandits on their heels. Finally, he turned his gaze to the east. The desert lay out there too, but more distant than to the south. Here the country was broken up into an exceptionally rugged and inhospitable terrain. The wide sluggish river swept around in a great curve there, the water brilliant and glittering in the sunlight.

He had already made up his mind what to do. They would ford the river – at this time of the year it was very low – and then head for the long, saddle-backed ridge which looked down upon the gulch about a mile away. By nightfall, if all went well, they should all be in position. After that, a lot depended on Gonzales and his men.

He allowed his thoughts to trickle through his mind. It was possible that the bandit band had made slow progress across the desert and were still several miles away to the south-east, that they would not reach the gulch by night-fall and would camp up somewhere further on in the desert. On the other hand, they might decide to ride around the southernmost limits of the spread and move far to the south, linking up with Wicker and his gang before attacking. So much seemed to be dependent upon one man – Gonzales, the Mexican bandit chief.

There was a sudden call from behind him and he turned instantly. One of the men was pointing a finger towards the south. Shading his eyes against the strong sunlight, Bret managed to make out the dark mass, just visible in the distance.

'Riders,' said Redden softly. 'A lot of men and heading this way – fast.'

'They're Gonzales and his gang,' said Bret thinly. 'Couldn't possibly be anyone else; not coming from that direction and kicking up so much dust.'

'Then we'd better hit the trail again.'

Bret nodded. He estimated that the riders were still many miles away. It would be a couple of hours before they reached the vicinity of the gulch. Nodding in satisfaction, he leapt into the saddle again, waited for the others to do likewise, checking his guns. His face was hard and set into lines of grim determination. Every nerve and instinct screamed at him to act. But he fought down the feeling. There was undoubtedly the necessity for urgency, that was true, but also caution if they were to stand any chance of survival at all.

When one was outnumbered like this, strategy was essential. Swiftly, they edged their mounts down the narrow, winding trail, descending to the valley floor. Down there, in the valley, the tall bluffs hid them completely from anyone advancing from the south and they made good time until they reached the gulch where their progress was slowed by the uneven nature of the ground. Here they left their mounts where they would be suffi-ciently distant from the fighting and yet close enough for a quick get-away.

'Tell all of the men to get into the rocks and be ready for my signal,' hissed Bret. 'Nobody is to open fire until they hear it.' Without waiting for a reply, he slithered into the rocks, climbing to the top of the ridge where he could look down into the wilderness which lay beyond. Bret saw that he had timed things nicely. The bunch of riders were now almost a mile away in the fast fading light and already they were circling as they neared the gulch. He doubted now if they would advance any further until dawn. For all they knew, the whole of Sundown might be ranged against them in the woods to the north-west.

For almost an hour he lay crouched among the rocks, watching the scene below as the light faded and night came creeping swiftly over the prairie. It was obvious that the men down there were supremely confident of themselves. The idea that they might, in turn, be attacked must have been far from their thoughts as they began to build fires and cook some food.

Bret noticed with a feeling of satisfaction, that most of their horses had been herded together into a natural corral among the rocks where there was a little coarse grass. It ought not to be too difficult, he reflected, for a man to creep down there in the darkness and stampede them.

He crawled back to the others. 'Well, Bret?' muttered Redden. 'How do things look out there? Pretty bad, I guess.'

'Could be worse, I suppose.' He deliberately kept his voice low although the nearest of the bandits was well over a quarter of a mile away. 'They've no idea that we're so close. And they have most of their mounts penned into an open space among the rocks.'

'Just what do you have in mind, Bret?'

'I'm going down there to scatter those horses once it gets really dark. Once you hear the shots open fire with the rifles. We can't hope to wipe out all of them but in the confusion it should be possible to kill some of them with few casualties to ourselves. Without their horses, they'll be helpless.'

'OK. Bret. We're all with you. But be careful. If you're seen, it would mean the end – not only for you, but of everything we're trying to do.'

'Don't worry. I'll keep my eyes open every inch of the way. They may have a guard posted down there to watch the horses. If there is, I'll have to take care of him without making a noise.' He pulled the long-bladed hunting knife from its sheath, ran the ball of his thumb along the razor-sharp edge. The smile on his face had a wolfish quality about it.

Like a shadow, he melted into the rocks as the others settled down behind their rifles to wait. His boots made only the barest whisper of sound on the rocks as he slid forward into the gloom. The horses were restless and he was forced to pause several times as they skittered noisily around in the open space where they had been penned. There was a patch of tall grass on a hump of earth overlooking the horses and he made for it with an Indian-like stealth.

He had almost reached it when he stopped, every movement frozen into immobility, his heart thudding wildly in his chest. The dark figure which had suddenly moved out of the shadows was so close that he could almost reach out and touch him. Slitting his eyes, Bret watched tensely, taking in every detail of the guard. The man was short and stocky with a drooping moustache and hard eyes. There was a bandoleer around his shoulders and chest and a rifle laid carelessly over his knees. His head was tilted back a little and he stared out into the night sky like a man just carved from stone.

Scarcely daring to breathe, Bret slipped the knife from its sheath. At any moment, the other might turn his head from the silent contemplation of the sky and see him crouching there. Only a few inches separated him from the guard now. Suddenly the man moved. Bret poised himself to lunge forward with the knife upraised, then paused as he saw that the man had turned away from him, was looking down to where the others were camped. Evidently the other was debating whether or not to go down for food, leaving the horses unguarded. If that happened, thought Bret, it would simplify matters a lot. But the other suddenly shrugged his shoulders and seated himself on the rock once again, fingers curled around the butt of the rifle.

Seconds later, the guard not knowing that death was so close, Bret stepped up behind him, a grim and relentless figure, the knife upraised in his right hand. Savagely, he struck, the blade slicing through the man's shirt and flesh just above the right lung. He pitched forward without a moan as it entered his heart. With his free hand, Bret caught the rifle before it fell. Gently, he eased the man's body into the rocks, out of sight, then moved swiftly, knowing that there were only a few seconds left before the bandits became suspicious. One of the horses whinnied loudly as he rolled aside the rocks which had been placed in position and slipped inside the corral. He noticed that most of the horses there had been tethered together, possibly as precaution against one or two of them straying during the night.

With the rocks removed, he climbed swiftly away from the danger of flying hoofs, then fired his Colt three times in rapid succession. In the confined space among the rocks, the noise was deafening, the echoes chasing themselves along the narrow cleft. Rearing and neighing, the horses jostled around in a mêlée for a few moments, then plunged out through the opening he had made, stampeding down the gulch. From the valley below, came the sound of excited voices. Bret paused for a moment to make sure that the horses were well away, then clambered back to rejoin the others.

'Nice work, Bret,' said Redden. 'I figger that ought to hold them there for a while. It'll be morning now before they catch most of those horses.' He fired at a running figure that tried to clamber up the rocky face of the gulch. The man uttered a shrill scream and fell back, on top of another man moving up below. They both went down in a sprawling heap, and only one got to his feet and began limping away as quickly as his legs would carry him.

'We'll have to keep our eyes open, make sure that none of them work their way around the gulch and steal our horses,' called Bret loudly, to make himself heard above the almost continual chatter of gunfire.

'I've already got one of the boys back there, keeping a look out for any trick like that. We'll get plenty of warning if they try it.'

'Good.' Bret rested the barrel of his rifle on a rocky ledge, squinted along the sights and squeezed the trigger as he caught a glimpse of two men rushing forward past one of the brightly burning fires. For a brief instant, their silhouettes showed up clearly against the flickering flames. Then one stumbled as if he had missed his footing in the sand and fell headlong. His companion stood hesitant for a moment, staring down at him, then ran forward for a couple of yards before Bret's second bullet hit him.

Gradually, the number of men visible down in the valley dwindled away as the bandits sought cover among the rocks. They had recovered swiftly from their surprise and were firing steadily and accurately into the gulch. Bret ducked his head in reflex action as a bullet hummed through the air close by and ricocheted off the rock behind him.

'I reckon that sooner or later, they're going to try to rush us,' whispered Redden, pressing his lips close to Bret's ear. 'What then? Our fire won't hold them for long.'

'I'm going down there again,' hissed Bret, lowering his rifle to the ground in front of him and checking his Colts. 'I've an idea they may try to slip up the trail back there and from here we can't see them. Keep firing until I get back.' Keeping his head low, he moved down the narrow trail, sliding from shadow to shadow, ears alert for the faintest sound in front of him which would tell him of the approach of any of the enemy.

Not until he had gone almost twenty yards did he hear anything. The men were coming quickly up the trail, scorning cover. Bret waited until they were almost, level with him before firing. The first five men died instantly, rifles thudding to the rocks. The others paused for a moment, then turned and fled in confusion.

He fired a couple of shots after them, thought he heard

a dull groan from one of the fleeing men, then paused to examine the bodies lying in the middle of the trail. They were all dead and he dragged them by their bandannas to one side. He waited there for several minutes, tensed, but there was no other sound and he guessed that they had given up the idea of sneaking up on them like that; at least for the time being.

More firing had flared up from below when he got back to the others. The bandits had now realized that there were only a handful of men facing them and they were relying on sheer weight of numbers to crush any resistance. But Bret had chosen their defensive position well. To reach it, the enemy had to cross several yards of open ground, after climbing a particularly difficult stretch of rock. In the dimness, he could see several dark bodies littered along the rock slopes and there was a rising exultation within him, a feeling that even though they were so desperately outnumbered they had not been out-fought. They were still holding the enemy, still keeping him at bay. And Gonzales was operating a long way from his own stamping grounds. He could not replace the men he'd lost, even in a skirmish like this.

A bunch of men rose up out of the darkness at the bottom of the gulch and came running forward, firing from the hip. Swiftly, Bret brought up his two Colts and added his firepower to the thunderous crash of the rifles. Then men continued to fire for almost a minute, then broke and ran for cover.

'We must have killed over a score of the varmints,' grunted one of the men hoarsely. 'Yet they still keep coming on. At this rate, there won't be many of them left for the others to get their teeth into tomorrow.'

'Don't fool yourself,' said Bret seriously, snapping a shot at two men who broke cover and ventured inside killing range of his Colts. 'There are plenty more men out there, and pretty soon they'll get wise to our position here and either draw off and reform out there in the desert before coming in and overwhelming us by sheer weight of numbers; or they'll simply pull back, catch their horses and wait until morning. In the daylight we don't stand much of a chance.'

'You aiming to pull out before morning, Bret?' It was more of a statement than a question and Bret nodded. 'We have to,' he said tersely. 'By then, they'll have got most of their horses back. I know those horses. They're trained to return after an hour or so. Another hour at the most and then we light out of here and back to the ranch. We'll make sure that they follow us though, otherwise this will have been for nothing.'

He lifted his head and peered down the rocky slope. 'Looks as if they've veered off,' he said after a pause, his mouth set into a tight line. 'Either that or they're waiting for us to show ourselves.'

He sat back with his shoulders resting against the hard, cold rock, eyes peering into the darkness in front of him. His skin was prickling a little and he had the feeling that there was a plan being built up against them at this very moment although he could not guess at what it was. He wondered about that solitary guard that Redden had set to watch the horses, remembering the way in which he, himself, had killed that Mexican who was performing exactly the same task for Gonzales. If it could happen to him, why not to the man they had sent back. The conviction that something was happening back there grew so strong within him that he half rose to his feet and Redden glanced at him sharply out of the corner of his eye.

'Something wrong. Bret? You look jumpy. I've never seen you quite like this.'

'I've got a feeling there's something wrong. It isn't like killers to stop shooting in the middle of a fight, particularly after so many of them have been killed. I would have expected them to come swarming over the rocks to get at us, yelling for our blood.'

'Could be they're reforming for another attack out

there. They've kicked out all of the fires.'

'Maybe. But I don't think so. They must realize by now that they'll lose a lot more men if they try another frontal attack and Gonzales isn't a fool – far from it. He'll know that Wicker has lost a lot of men trying to do something just like this and he isn't likely to fall into the same kind of trap.' He fought to still the little germ of panic that was shrieking in the back of his mind. The muscles of his stomach were hardened into a tight knot and he realized that his fingers were gripping the butts of the guns more tightly than usual. With a conscious physical and mental effort, he forced himself to relax. Not a sound came from the gulch which lay in darkness in front of them. Occasionally, there came the sharp bark of a rifle from among the rocks near at hand, but he guessed that whoever it was, was firing at shadows rather than at some definitely seen target. He licked his lips drily and tried to make out shapes from the angled contours of the ground all around him. Were there more men working their way up along the trail, moving more stealthily this time, taking care to make no noise? Or were they some distance away, grouping together, planning their next move now that they had run into trouble far sooner than they had expected? Or were they already beginning to work their way around the gulch, to take them from the rear?

It was the last possibility that worried him the most. Half an hour passed and still there was no move from the men in the gulch.

'Surely to God those varmints haven't drawn off?' muttered one of the men in a dry, throaty whisper. He lifted his head and peered over the rocks. 'No, goddammit, I can see some of them moving around down there and —'

His words were punctuated by the sharp bark of a gun down in the gulch and a second later, he reeled back from the rocks and collapsed on to the ground less than three feet from where Bret lay.

Swiftly, he crawled over to the other, bent to examine him more closely then saw with a sick certainty that there was nothing he could do for the man. Whoever had fired that shot had been an excellent marksman. The bullet had ploughed a ragged-edged hole between the man's eyes, killing him instantly.

'At least we know that some of them are still there,' grunted Redden. 'That was a fool thing to do anyway, showing himself like that.'

'They're probably all down there in a huddle right this minute,' said another man from the shadows. 'They're figuring on a way to prise us out of here without losing too many men in the process.'

'I only wish it was as simple as that. Sure they've had a plastering, but not enough to stop them coming in again. But this time, they'll try something a little different. They'll send one group around to the rear, either to get at our mounts or to take us by surprise. It doesn't matter which they do, it could be a dangerous move. We've got to be ready to pull out before they can do anything like that. I know it sounds as if we're running away just at the moment when we seem to be getting on top of them, but there's no point in taking unnecessary chances with these killers. We'll be needed back there at the ranch tomorrow. They've killed one man.' He nodded towards the body lying near his feet, 'and we need every gun we can get when the showdown comes.'

The men fell silent. If there were any who dissented from his view, they gave no outward sign. A few more shots were fired down into the darkness, then Bret gave the word to pull out. The feeling of impending disaster was still strong within him, but when they scrambled down the rocks at the back of the ridge, they found the guard still there, watchful, and the horses champing nervously in the darkness.

Mounting swiftly, they headed away from the ridge, back along the way they had come. In the darkness it was difficult to ride fast; and besides, there was little point in it if they wanted the bandits to follow their trail rather than turn and head for the town. Bret deliberately held a slow pace, pausing every so often to listen for the sound of pursuit. Finally, they heard it, the distance drumming of hoof-beats behind them, the sound of many horses.

'Sounds to me as though you were right about those horses being trained,' said Redden. 'They're coming. It'll be light in a little while and then it won't be difficult to follow our trail.'

'And with luck it ought to lead them to their own destruction,' said Bret. He did not feel quite as confident as he tried to sound. The skirmish back there at the gulch had succeeded beyond his wildest dreams. It had been impossible to estimate in the darkness how many of the Mexican outlaws had been killed but it was certainly well over a score; and apart from them, others must have been so badly wounded that they could no longer be counted in the fighting force.

But there were still Wicker's men to be taken into consideration. They would more than compensate for those of Gonzales's band who had been killed. Together, they still made up an overwhelming force which only a miracle could help to defeat. Presently, they crossed the boundary fence and entered the southern end of the spread. Here they were on more familiar ground and progress was a little more rapid. They linked up with the rest of the men two hours later, just as dawn was beginning to streak the eastern horizon.

Swiftly, Bret slid from the saddle and dropped down beside the men. They looked at him curiously.

'They're right behind us,' he said briskly, 'about half an hour's ride away. We killed several of them, but it's still quite a sizeable force. Any sign of Wicker and his bunch?'

'We've seen nothing of them,' grunted one of the men harshly. He shifted his position a little. 'Could be that he knows nothing of this. If that's the case, he may be waiting back at the Lazy V and to all intents and purposes we've split their force.'

Bret nodded as he looked about him. The men were spread out behind a natural defensive position which had been strengthened by several walls of rock set up so that a withering crossfire could be brought to bear upon the attackers without any of the defenders having to expose themselves. In the circumstances, it was the best they had been able to do. He had no illusions about what would happen when Gonzales finally arrived with his men. They could hold them there for a little while, but in the end, they would be forced back to the ranch itself. There, they would have to make their last stand.

He rolled himself a cigarette and carefully shielding the match from the cool wind, he lit it and drew gratefully on it. His nerves and limbs were still taut and stiff and his mind was working furiously, trying to think ahead, to put himself in the place of the Mexican bandit, to figure out what he was likely to do in the circumstances. It had been essential that they should bring the other to battle on ground of their own choosing. Here, the other's superiority in numbers, was minimized as much as possible by the terrain. They could only approach from the front. The flanks were both well guarded and anyone trying to attack from those directions would come under a murderous hail of fire.

Redden got to his feet and began to move up and down behind the rocks, his arms swinging loosely by his sides. Bret watched him closely as he inhaled the pungent smoke from the cigarette. The other was nervy and on edge. It was only to be expected after what they had been through that night, and facing the almost certain prospect of having his ranch and this spread taken away from under his very nose, possibly of even being killed before the day was through. All of these combined to make him nervous and tensed.

The minutes dragged on. The enemy were somewhere

behind them, but so far they could see no sign of them. Possibly Gonzales had decided to be a little more cautious now. He had perhaps been relying on attacking first and gaining the initiative. But that had been lost now. The element of surprise too had gone, had been snatched from him by their attack during the night. The best he could hope for now, would be to advance slowly and attack from under cover, sweeping in when the defenders least expected it.

Leaning his back and shoulders against the rocky wall, Bret glanced along at the others. They too, were tensed. There seemed to be an electric tautness which communicated itself from one man to another. Every sudden and untoward movement was sufficient to bring them jerkily upright, hands grasping their rifles, heads lifted, eyes narrowed.

'Why the devil don't they come and get it over with?' grunted Redden, sinking down beside Bret. 'It's this goddarned waiting that's beginning to get on my nerves.'

'Could be that Gonzales is planning it this way. He knows that we're here, waiting for him, and he wants everything to be on his side when he does come in to the attack. He recognizes the fact that this is a strongly defended position and he wants to save as many of his men as possible to help him sack Sundown. There's also one other possibility that has occurred to me and I guess Gonzales has thought about it too.'

Redden raised his brows. 'What's that?' he asked curiously.

Bret smiled faintly. 'They always say that there's honour among thieves, but in this case, I doubt it. I've a feeling that neither man really trusts the other and Gonzales wants to be sure that he has enough men to back him in any play he may have to make against Wicker. My guess is that Wicker will hold off until Gonzales has made his play against us. If we succeed in destroying most of the Mexican force, then he'll have a chance to move in and take over. He'll be the ultimate victor.'

'That's something I hadn't considered,' murmured the other thoughtfully. 'Playing the two sides off against each other, making certain that way, that no matter which one wins he will be able to move in and smash all opposition.'

'It's a pity that Gonzales is such a vicious killer, otherwise we might have stood a chance of convincing him of that.'

'There they are,' said one of the men sharply, his voice rising a little in pitch.

As one man, they all turned to where the sun was just rising over the pine-covered hills to the east. The small dots which had appeared on the skyline were clearly visible and even as they watched, the distant riders spurred their horses and rode down towards the valley.

'All right, men,' said Bret crisply. 'You all know what to do. We have to stop them here for as long as possible. We've got plenty of ammunition, but make every shot count. And above all, keep your eyes peeled for any sign of Wicker and his men from the Lazy V. They may try to attack us from the rear and if that happens, we'll have to get out of here in a goddarned hurry.'

In a few moments, the oncoming group of men became more distinct. Bret could make out the individual riders now; the dots took on a semblance of shape as they came closer, moving forward in a wide arc to attack on as wide a front as possible.

'Hold your fire until I give the word,' he yelled. The thunder of hoofs in the distance could just be heard now. 'They're still well out of range.'

The men lay tensed behind their rifles. Bret watched the play of emotions over Redden's face. More than anyone else, he stood to lose everything in this attack. Even if he were not killed in the fighting, the chances of him losing the ranch and everything it contained, were very high, far higher than Bret had cared to admit, even to himself. There seemed no end to the riders approaching from the east. They entered the pine belt and vanished from sight for a little while.

Tightening his lips, Bret waited for them to reappear out of the trees. Once they came out into the open again, they would be almost within killing range of the high-powered rifles, although too far for Colts to give any real effect. He had roughly estimated the mounted men to number between sixty and seventy.

They waited in breathless expectancy. Then the vanguard of the raiders burst out through the trees and even from that distance, they could hear the savage yells of the men as they swept forward into the wide sweep of the trail.

Bret waited until the leading men were less than two hundred yards away, then gave the order to fire. Instantly, every rifle along the defensive position spat fire. The full devastating effect of that volley, poured in at close range was almost immediate.

Several men went down, falling from the saddles as the bullets found their mark. There was instant confusion. The outlaws must have known where the defences were but they had come thundering on blindly and had run into that withering blast of fire. Horses reared violently, throwing their riders. Another volley rang out and added more confusion.

7
Showdown

The main force of outlaws dismounted while just beyond range of the rifles and went under cover, slapping their mounts to get them out of the way. This was what Bret had feared. He had hoped that they would have been able to kill a few more of the Mexicans before they got under cover. At least a dozen men lay in the grass, unmoving, and closer at hand a horse which had been shot lay on its side, kicking feebly with its legs.

Behind the men, Bret could see a tall man with a thin, cruel hawklike face and a brilliant red sash around his middle. He guessed that this was Gonzales himself, the leader of these men. He sighted his rifle instinctively on the sash and squeezed the trigger, but the other had been careful to keep well out of range and the bullet fell short.

The firing slackened a little on both sides. For a moment, there was stalemate with each side under cover. But the Mexicans were in the more dangerous position. There was little cover for them out there on the trail, apart from a few scattered patches of tall grass. Here and there a man suddenly rose to his feet and tried to run forward, only to be picked off by a rifle bullet before he had taken half a dozen paces. Bret could hear movement in the

142

distance, the furtive sounds of men slipping back to the safety of the trees. He eased himself back a little. For the moment, the enemy would keep under cover until they had figured out a way to get around their position.

'They may try to outflank us,' he called so that everyone could hear. 'Keep a close watch out there and shoot at anything that moves. Anybody been hurt?'

A quick check disclosed that no one had been hit, that few of the enemy had been using rifles and most of their fire had fallen short.

'We've quieted them for a little while,' he said grimly. 'I spotted Gonzales a few minutes ago, back there among the trees. Obviously he doesn't intend to take any chances at getting himself killed. Pretty soon, he's going to give the order to his men to move forward. They'll try to overrun us, coming at us from three sides. You can see them moving across into position out there, keeping well out of range.'

'We've held 'em so far,' gritted one of the men nearby. 'I figger we can hold them, even if they do try to rush us.'

'I hope so. If they do try, use your rifles so long as they're out of range of your Colts, then use them. Don't waste time trying to reload the rifles. It will be too late by then.'

Firing started up again from the direction of the trees. Some of it thudded among the rocks and stones behind which they lay. Bret rightly assessed that it was designed to make them keep their heads down while the rest of the men moved up into fresh positions. Very carefully, he lifted his head until he could see through a narrow gap in the stones. A small group of enemy dashed forward and then sank down out of sight in a small hollow less than a hundred yards away. Even as they went to ground, another group, a little further back ran forward and repeated the procedure. So that was how they meant to attack, he thought grimly.

Some of the other defenders had seen this move too,

for the next time a small cluster of Mexicans rose to their feet they were met by a withering hail of rifle fire and not one of them got more than two or three paces before being hit.

There was an uneasy silence for a long moment after that abortive attempt to get closer to their positions. It was a deep and clinging silence that was soon broken by a fusillade of fire from the trees. Simultaneously, close on fifty men rose up out of the long grass and ran forward, firing as they came. They swung in from three sides in a wild arc. Bret killed two of them with the rifle, then heard the hammer click on a empty chamber and threw it down instantly, pulling the Colts from their holsters. Lifting himself slightly, scorning the bullets that zipped and shrieked around him, he fired swiftly and instinctively, scarcely seeming to take aim, yet almost every bullet found its mark.

Two men got within ten feet of the low wall, suddenly leapt up into the air in an attempt to clear it and died in mid-air as Bret shifted his aim slightly. They crashed down on top of the wall, their bodies spread-eagled across it, arms outflung, the revolvers falling from their hands, their eyes glazed in death, staring sightlessly over the wall at the position they had tried to capture.

Grimly, relentlessly, Bret continued to fire at running, yelling men. Something scorched across his shoulder and for a moment his right arm went numb as if a red-hot poker had been applied to his flesh. Flattened against the wall, he fired again and again into the horde of men that came rushing blindly towards them.

Rifle fire was still stabbing the dimness under the distant trees, very fast now. Two men, along the line of defenders suddenly threw up their arms, their bodies arched as they reeled back, falling to the ground to lie still. Bret gave them a cursory glance, then turned his attention back to the front.

The Colt .45s were booming now all along the line,

their fire louder and less sharp than the bark of the rifles. The raiders began edging in, some keeping their heads low, others running forward as though convinced that they bore charmed lives. A man screamed in mortal agony as Bret fired twice and as he dropped, Bret saw that the man was a Mexican half-breed. He wondered vaguely where the two men were who had been sent to fetch Gonzales. He had seen no sign of them so far and the possibility came to him that perhaps they had ridden off to warn Wicker of what was happening.

He reloaded his Colts, crouching down behind the wall listening to the bullets smacking against it with dull, leaden thuds or shrieking off into the distance as they ricocheted off the unyielding stone. More of the ranch hands had been hit, he saw, as he lifted himself again. Two were lying slumped against the wall with blood staining their shirts. Very soon, he reflected, if the attack continued to be pressed home with this terrible and insane fury on the part of the Mexicans, they would have to seriously consider the possibility of pulling out. It was not going to be as easy as it had been back at the gulch. Here, they would be forced to expose themselves to rapid and accurate fire and the enemy had their mounts ready too among the trees.

He lifted himself slightly, aiming the Colts, then turned with a sudden oath as the man next to him suddenly caught at his arm, spoiling his aim.

'More of them, coming up on our flank,' hissed the other urgently. 'Looks to me like Wicker and his gang. They must have heard the ruckus and come along to investigate. We don't stand any chance now.'

Bret sucked in his breath sharply. Even from that distance, there was no difficulty in recognizing the Lazy V hands. This was what he had dreaded all along. Attacked from both sides, it was only a question of time before he and his little band were totally annihilated. He cast about him desperately, trying to gauge how long it would be before the others arrived on the scene. Already, the Mexicans had spotted them, had realized who they were, and were pressing home their attack with a savage, redoubled ferocity.

Swiftly, Bret crammed fresh shells into the Colts, ignoring the pain in his shoulder. One glance had been enough to tell him that the bullet had merely ploughed a deep, red furrow through the flesh and glanced off the bone, that the wound looked more dangerous than it really was. He came back into the fire just as Redden finished his last round and ducked down behind the wall. Carefully, he lifted his head and fired at running men. In the distance, he could just make out the brilliant red sash which Gonzales wore around his middle. To their right, Wicker and his men rode up, some throwing lead as they came, although for the most part they were still out of range.

This was what Gonzales had obviously been waiting for, the linking of the two groups. Now they were confident of victory. He felt a sudden overwhelming sense of defeat rising up within him. This was surely the end, the end of everything of the plans which these people had made, of the labours they had carried out since they had arrived at Sundown. Time could bring nothing but victory for the powers of lawlessness and evil.

But still, something continued to drive him on, even though he knew now that the position was completely hopeless. Nothing short of a miracle could prevent disaster now, and in the past it had been his experience that miracles did not just happen, they had to be engineered.

'It ain't no use staying here to be slaughtered,' shouted one of the men, suddenly rising to his feet. 'They'll ride us down now that Wicker has joined forces with them.' The man began waving his arms wildly and Bret lurched forward in a savage movement, caught him about the waist and pulled him down behind the cover of the stones.

'Just keep still, you fool,' he hissed thinly. 'Unless you want to get yourself killed. Everything isn't lost yet. We're still in a strong position and they've lost almost a quarter of their men already. We'll begin pulling back towards the ranch once there's a lull in the firing. To attempt to move now would be suicide.'

'We can't stay here,' gasped the other, squirming in an attempt to free himself from Bret's iron grip. 'You've got us into this trap, now you'll have to get us out of it.'

'Panic isn't going to help at all,' snarled Bret. There was a savage anger deep within him now. He had expected something like this when things got a little too tough, but once started, panic could sweep through the whole group of men and it would be difficult, if not impossible to stop.

Leaving Redden with the man, Bret checked the chambers of his sixers, filled them quickly with slugs from his belt, then circled back to his right to join the men at the end of the line.

'How are things here?' he asked tightly.

'Pretty tough, Bret,' muttered one of the men. His face was tight and lined with strain. 'Things don't look too hopeful now, do they? Was that Wicker and his gang who just rode up?'

'Afraid so. At least we know what we're up against. They'll attack in a few minutes. Just keep up a steady fire, make every shot count, and wait for the signal to mount up and pull back to the ranch. We'll make our last stand there.'

It was an unfortunate choice of words, he knew, but at the moment, he could think of little else to say. The cards were stacked against them now, had been from the very beginning of this deal. It seemed that Fate was determined to remain against them.

He fired a single shot at one of the half-breeds who came running out of the long grass, saw the man stumble, one hand clutching at his chest as he rolled over and then lay still. It seemed to be such a futile gesture, that killing of one man, he thought tiredly. A sudden shout jerked him back to the present.

Glancing up he saw, to his surprise, that two men were walking towards them from the direction of the trees. One held a white cloth on a piece of stick over his head. The other man was Darby Wicker. Both men appeared to be unarmed.

'This could be a trick,' yelled Bret sharply. 'Keep your guns on them both, but don't fire until we hear what they have to say.'

He waited until the two men had approached to within fifteen yards of their positions, then got cautiously to his feet and called: 'That's far enough, Wicker. Speak your piece from there and no tricks mind.'

'Manders. I thought it would be you.' There was a cruel amusement in the other's tone. 'I came here to speak to the men with you.' He turned his head and allowed his gaze to travel along the line of grim, determined men. 'I've got little quarrel with most of you,' he called loudly, 'only with men like Manders there and Redden who refused to accept a fair offer for their ranches. I'm not a hard man, but if you don't accept this, my last offer, all of you, then you'll be wiped out. I don't think you need any more proof of that than to look over there at the force ranged against you. You can't hope to stand up against those men. If I give the order to them to advance, you'll be annihilated.'

'Just what is it you want, Wicker?' shouted one of the men hoarsely.

'Simply this. You go back to your homes and I promise that you'll not be troubled any further. All I want are three men; Manders, Redden and Nolan. The rest of you can go free. Is that a fair enough offer for you?'

'Your smooth talk won't work here, Wicker,' shouted Bret as he saw some of the men beginning to waver at the other's honeyed tone. 'We all know what you're like. Once you get rid of the only men who have dared to stand against you, then you'll start on the others. Nobody in the whole territory will be safe until you and that killer behind you are finished. Everyone here knows what happened the last time Gonzales was here. They haven't forgotten the burned buildings in Sundown, the men and women and children who were massacred by his band of cut-throats. Once you've finished with us, the same thing will happen again.'

'Don't listen to him' called Wicker sharply. 'Those are the kind of words you'd expect from a man who's going to die. Consider my offer carefully. Three men against the rest of you. If you refuse, I promise you that not one of you will live to see the night.'

'At least we'll die as free men, Wicker,' said Redden loudly. He brought up his gun but Bret knocked it down swiftly. 'Let him go back to his bandit friends,' he said loudly, so that everyone could hear. 'He's under a flag of truce, something which we respect, although I doubt whether he would.'

Wicker remained standing for a few moments, looking up and down the line of grim-faced men; then when no one made any move, he turned sharply on his heel and stalked back through the grass. He paused, only once to yell: 'This is the end of you all. Within an hour I promise that you'll all be buzzard-meat.'

Bret watched him go with a sinking feeling in the pit of his stomach. There was a feeling of pride in his mind at the way the other men had turned down Wicker's offer. He would not have been surprised if most of them had accepted it. But they had all stood firm and —

'Bret! Look over there!' cried Redden, pointing to the south. Far up the valley, a lone horseman was riding on the skyline, perhaps a mile away. Even at that distance, Bret could see that he carried a rifle.

'More of 'em – on foot.' Redden's voice was little more than a whisper. A sharp fusillade of shots rang out from the trees across the trail, but Bret scarcely noticed them. Down over the ridge in the distance, poured an avalanche of men, armed men. It took several seconds for Bret to

realize the full significance of what had happened and
even then his mind had difficulty in taking it in. Somehow,
the miracle he had prayed for had been engineered for
him and he could make a guess at who had been responsible. Only one person could have so shamed the men of
Sundown, the ordinary citizens and the homesteaders –
Fay Saunders.

As they approached, he estimated that there must have
been close on three hundred men, more than enough to
turn the tide of battle in their favour. 'All right, boys,' he
yelled jubilantly. 'Let them have it. We've got them pinned
down now.'

In the valley, several of the raiders had spotted the
horde of men advancing swiftly towards them and were
running for their horses. Fighting a small force of armed
men, pinned down behind a handful of stone barricades
was one thing, but facing up to an angry mob which
outnumbered them by more than five to one, was another;
a proposition which they did not relish. Men on foot were
scrambling up from their hiding places, trying to reach
their horses. Swiftly, Bret ran forward over the barricade,
shouting to the others to follow him. Many of the half-
breeds would try to head over the Mexican border; but he
guessed that few of them would make it. Those that the
desert did not claim would be hunted down like animals
by the townsfolk. There was going to be a cleaning up in
this frontier territory, he thought delightedly. He watched
as the men came in swiftly, firing as they advanced. A few
of the outlaws attempted to make a stand, but were swiftly
overwhelmed. Others climbed into the saddle, pulled
their horses round savagely and spurred them back
towards the distant ridge.

The firing flared up into a new intensity, then began to
die down again as the last of the survivors were mopped
up. Going forward, Bret examined several of the bodies.
Among the trees, half-buried in the thick undergrowth, he
found the body of Gonzales. He still carried his guns in his

hands and the brilliant red sash now blended well with the crimson on his shirt.

'He won't be troubling us any more,' said Redden quietly. There was a broad smile on his face, the first that Bret had seen for several days. 'It still doesn't seem possible that this could really have happened.'

'It's real all right,' declared Bret. 'Once we get the rest of these outlaws rounded up, I suggest that we ride into town and try to sort things out. I doubt whether Veldon will be in the sheriff's office for long.'

As they rode into Sundown, Bret could sense a new feeling in the air. It was nothing tangible, but something which could be sensed all the same. There was only one thing on his mind now, one thing which troubled him more than he cared to admit. Although they had searched all of the men who had been killed or captured during the fighting on the Redden spread, there had been no sign of Darby Wicker, the man who had been the brains behind it all. Somehow, the other had got clean away in the confusion. Possibly he had ridden with the survivors of the Gonzales gang and was even now heading for the Mexican border as fast as his horse would carry him. Bret wrinkled his forehead in concentration. Somehow, that was not in line with Wicker's character as he knew it of old. The man might run out on his men if the battle turned against him. He thought too much of his precious skin to do otherwise. But he was no coward. He would not leave Sundown or the Lazy V ranch unless it was absolutely necessary to save his life.

Bret had dispatched a small force of men to the Lazy V ranch with orders to search the entire place for him. In the meantime, he had men scouring Sundown but so far without any success.

He hitched his stallion to the rail in front of the sheriff's office and went inside. Veldon was there, standing in one corner. A crowd of homesteaders were also in the room, tough-looking men. They turned as Bret came in and gave a quick nod of recognition. 'Looks like we were just in time back there,' said one of them in a friendly voice. 'I reckon we've seen the last of them.'

'I certainly hope so,' said Bret gravely. He walked over to Veldon and grabbed him by the shirt front, pulling him close. 'Do you know where Wicker has gone to earth, Sheriff?'

The other jerked his head back in terror and shook his head, eyes wide. 'I've never seen him since he rode out of town early this morning. He didn't come back and I figured that he'd managed to wipe you all out. Then the homesteaders came back and I got some of the story from them. I was all set to come out and help, but scarcely anyone knew where you were holed up.'

'I'll bet you were,' sneered Bret. He flung the other from him so that the sheriff hit the wall and slid down to the floor in an ungainly heap. 'I guess you won't be sheriff in this town much longer. Pretty soon, when things get organized, you'll be lookin' for a new job.'

The other said nothing, but sat there nursing his shoulder where it had struck the wall. Bret turned to the homesteaders. 'Did you get anything at all out of him? Wicker has got to be found wherever he is. But when he is found, I want him alive. He belongs to me.'

'He's made a lot of enemies here,' said another of the men harshly. 'There are quite a heap of folks would just like to put a bullet into that snake's belly.'

'Mebbe so. But I want him. Spread the word around. I'll be over in the Golden Ace saloon if anybody wants me.'

He stepped out on to the boardwalk and stood for a moment looking up and down the main street. The sun was up and the heat devils were just beginning to shimmer at either end. There were quite a lot of folk out on the boardwalk and a number of horses tied to the posts in front of the saloon. He walked over slowly, pushed open the batwing doors and stepped inside. The guy with the derby hat playing the piano glanced up once, gave him a quick smile, and went on playing.

He made his way over to the bar. There was still a tensed feeling inside him like that of a coiled spring ready to unwind. The bartender pushed a glass towards him and filled it.

'Glad to have you back with us,' he said jovially. 'We heard what happened back there. Never thought I'd live to see the day that the homesteaders would ride up and face Wicker and his cut-throats.'

'It must have been Fay's doing,' said Bret, downing the drink. The raw spirit stung the back of his throat, then exploded inside his stomach in an expanding cloud of warmth. 'Where is she? I'd like to thank her for what she did.'

'Up in her room, I guess. She ought to have come down a little while ago.'

The fear which had been lurking at the back of Bret's mind for several hours suddenly crystallized into something more definite, more frightening. Pushing the glass back across the bar, he eased the guns slowly in their holsters and then made his way with a deliberate slowness towards the wide stairs leading up to the rooms on the top floor. He trod silently as he climbed until he reached the corridor at the top. All of the doors were closed and there was a deep silence over everything. Even the men down below seemed hushed as though they were aware that something momentous was about to happen, but still unsure of what it might be.

He had the feeling that Wicker was here somewhere; and if he was right, then the most logical place would be in Fay's room, possibly holding a gun on her. She might be his one passport out of Sundown alive and there was also the possibility that he had somehow discovered she was the person who had been tipping them off as to Wicker's plans.

The conviction that Wicker was there, in that second room, was so strong that he knew he could not possibly ignore it. He edged his way towards the door, then paused and called harshly: 'I know you're in there, Wicker. Open up before I come in shooting.'

There was a moment's complete silence, then Bret thought he heard a sudden muffled cry as if someone had tried to cry out a warning, but a hand had been clapped over their mouth before they had managed to get the words out. A second later, Wicker's voice reached him through the closed door: 'All right, Manders. I figured you might trail me here. But I've got the girl and if you make one wrong move, she's going to get it first. Do you understand, Manders?'

'Yes, I understand.' Bret's mind was whirling rapidly, throwing up one idea after another, but rejected them all instantly. Somehow, he had to get the other out of that room. It would take too long to burst the door down, even if he shot off the lock. It needed only a fraction of a second for the other to shoot the girl and knowing Wicker of old, that had not been an idle threat. He had meant every word of it.

'Sooner or later, you'll have to come out, Wicker,' he called harshly. 'And when you do, I'll be waiting.'

'Better move away from the door, Manders,' snarled the other. 'I'm coming out and the girl will be in front of me. If you try to go for your guns, she gets it in the back.'

Bret cast about him desperately. There seemed nothing he could do. Then, abruptly, he felt a touch on his arm and whirled to find Redden standing beside him. Without pausing the other indicated that he was to move away from the door back towards the stairs. As Bret complied, he saw Redden tiptoe noiselessly along the corridor, pressing his body into one of the doorways.

For the space of two thudding heartbeats nothing happened. Then the door of Fay's room opened slightly. Wicker called harshly: 'You still there, Manders? Answer me before I plug the girl.'

'I'm over here,' Bret called. 'At at the head of the stairs.'

'Good. Then keep your hands away from your guns. I'm coming out and the girl is with me. If you try any funny tricks, I swear I'll kill her. Seems she's been the one who supplied you with all of your information; who started to talk to the homesteaders and talked them into turning against me. She's been just a little too industrious.'

The door opened wider and a moment later, Fay Saunders was pushed unceremoniously into the corridor. Darby Wicker emerged a moment later, a heavy, long-barrelled pistol in his right hand, the tip of which was thrust heavily into the small of the girl's back. He grinned broadly as he saw Bret standing in the middle of the corridor, his hands hanging limply by his sides.

'I've always promised myself that I'd get you like that, Manders,' he said smoothly. 'It's been a dream of mine ever since I shot your father and mother, eight years ago. I knew you'd never rest until you found me. Well, here I am. Just what are you aiming to do about it?'

Bret knew that the other was deliberately goading him. Out of the corner of his eye he saw Redden inching forward, wondered just what was in the other's mind, knew that very soon he would have to make his play and that the girl's life depended upon his move being the right one.

'Still tongue-tied,' went on Wicker. 'I never thought you'd be like that. I always figured that you'd be down on your knees pleading for mercy.' He laughed thinly, his eyes unnaturally bright. Bret saw the finger, bar-straight on the trigger of the gun, whiten with the pressure he was exerting.

'You'll never get away with this, Wicker,' he said, forcing evenness into his voice. 'Down there are fifty men all thirsting for your blood. You may be able to kill five or six of them, but the others will get you; and they won't shoot you as I would. There'll be a lynching party tonight in the streets of Sundown.'

The other's smiled broadened. 'Somehow, I don't think so. And even if it did turn out to be true, I can assure you that you won't be alive to witness it.'

'That's what you think, Wicker.' Redden's voice broke in upon the silence that followed. 'Just turn around very slowly and face me.'

Instinctively, Wicker whirled, the gun in his hand thundered as he squeezed the trigger. Bret saw Redden stagger forward as the bullet smashed into his body. In the same instant, he leapt forward, caught the girl's arm and pulled her swiftly to one side. Already, Wicker was beginning to turn, lining up the gun on Bret's body. In that precise moment, his hands streaked down for the guns at his side, so swiftly that it was impossible for the eye to follow them. Three guns seemed to roar in unison. Bret felt the whistle of the bullet as it passed within an inch of his head, smacking into the plaster of the wall at his back.

Wicker stood upright for a long moment, his face devoid of expression. He tried to turn his head to stare at the girl lying at his feet, then something seemed to snap in his body and he drooped forward, bending at the knees, falling on to his face on the rich, red carpet.

Slowly, Fay rose to her feet as Bret took her arm. She turned instantly to where Redden lay against the wall, his face a deathly white. His hand was clasped to his chest and already there was blood beginning to ooze between his fingers.

He smiled weakly at Bret, 'Seems like I made a fool of myself once more,' he said feebly.

'Better let me take a look at that,' said Bret. His first glance had told him that it was serious. The heavy-calibre bullet had smashed through the collar bone but had not come out at the back and there was internal haemorrhage. He looked up at the girl. 'Get me some boiling water,' he said sharply. 'Hurry now. And get one of the men to bring in my bag from the saddle. There are some instruments in it I'll need. I'll have to operate to get that bullet out and then plug the wound to stop that bleeding.'

'Is he going to die?' she asked anxiously.

'Not if I can help it,' he said crisply. 'Now just hurry along and get those things for me, otherwise he will.'

He heard her running along the corridor and down the stairway as he bent and cut the other's bloodstained shirt away from his body. Redden tightened his lips as a spasm of pain passed through his body, then he relaxed against the wall. 'Sorry,' he said weakly. 'How bad is it?'

'Not so good, but I figure we can get it out. You've got a constitution as strong as a horse. You'll pull through, especially after my excellent doctoring.'

'After seeing you in action before, I'd sooner trust you than anyone else,' said the other, closing his eyes.

A few moments later, Fay came back with the boiling water in a dish, and behind her, the bartender hurried forward with the small black bag. He also carried a bottle in his hand which he held out to Redden. 'One of the best anaesthetics I know,' he said quietly. 'Take a good slug.'

Redden's lips twitched into a travesty of a smile as he tilted the bottle to his lips and took a deep swallow. He almost gagged on the strong liquor, then gave a quick nod. 'Right, Bret. Go ahead, I'm ready.'

'Sure. This is going to hurt like hell, but it'll soon be over once I can find that bullet.'

He took out the probe and inserted it carefully into the wound. If that bullet had pierced the lung, then things looked bad for the rancher. On the other hand, judging by the place where it had gone in, he guessed that it had just missed it and that being the case, the only problems were to locate it, extract it and then stanch the flow of blood.

It took almost seven minutes to find the bullet, lodged almost beneath the collar bone. As he withdrew it slowly, Redden gave a sudden gasp and his head fell back against the wall. Fay looked up at Bret with an expression of questioning horror in her eyes, but he shook his head. 'He's unconscious,' he said quietly.

'That's a good thing in a way. At least, he won't feel any pain.' He dropped the bullet on to the floor beside him, then began to plug the wound. Fortunately it was quite clean and he didn't think there was any great risk of infection. Provided the other rested and there was no recurrence of the internal haemorrhage, the other would be up and about again, in a few weeks. He finished bandaging the other's shoulder, then said quietly: 'Is there a bed where we can carry him? He's not in any fit state to go back to the ranch yet.'

'Take him into my room,' said Fay quietly. She rose to her feet and threw open the door. 'It's the least I can do. After all, he saved my life.'

'He saved both our lives,' said Bret soberly. Gently, he carried the rancher into the room and laid him on the bed. 'We'll undress him in a little while. Right now, he needs rest more than anything else and above all, we must keep him quiet and still. Any sudden movement or excitement could be fatal.'

'I'll see that he gets the best of attention,' promised Fay Saunders.

'I'm sure that you will.' Bret nodded. He made his way down the stairs and into the saloon. There was a group of men at the far end of the room, talking among themselves. They turned as they saw him enter, eyed him up and down for a moment so that he felt uncomfortable under their gaze, then one of them came over to him.

'Mr Manders. We've been discussing what is to happen in Sundown now that Wicker is dead and there is no longer fear of reprisals from across the border. For the first time, it ought to be possible to bring law and order into Sundown. This isn't always going to be a small frontier town, you know. Very soon, they'll be bringing the railroad through here, to link up with the new settlements in California and we'll occupy a strategic position in the territory. We're going to expand and I think you'll agree with my friends and myself that for this to happen it is essential that the law and order we now have should be maintained.'

Bret looked at the other with a faint expression of

bewilderment on his face. Then he nodded slowly. 'I guess so. But what has all this to do with me?'

The other coughed, clearing his throat. 'We – ah – have been talking this over among ourselves and we have decided that we need a strong man, an honest man, to replace Veldon as sheriff in Sundown. We're offering you that job if you care to take it.'

'Me?' Bret looked at the other in surprise. 'But you know nothing about me. I only arrived here a week or so ago. For all you know, I could be wanted by the law in half a dozen states.'

The other shrugged his massive shoulders. 'That may be so. But here we'll take a chance on that. I think I know an honest man when I see one, a decent citizen who would uphold the law in Sundown.'

There were murmurs of agreement from the other men. Bret looked from one to the other, still feeling bewildered. This was something he had never expected. Now that his work was finished, now that Wicker was dead, that he had fulfilled the vow he had made eight years before, he had intended riding out, moving west, perhaps towards California. Now these people had asked him to be their sheriff.

'I really don't know what to say,' he said feebly. 'I intended merely riding out tomorrow, heading west.'

'You're the best man for the job. We're all agreed on that,' said the fat man persuasively. 'The one thing we want to be sure of is that no other man like Darby Wicker can ever come here and bring lawlessness to Sundown again.'

'Well, if you put it like that, I don't exactly see how I can refuse,' said Bret.

'Then it's settled,' declared the other. He took Bret by the arm, led him out through the swinging doors, across the street and into the sheriff's office. Veldon looked up and an expression of fear crossed his fleshy features as he saw the deputation standing in front of him. Briskly, the fat man explained why they were there and to Bret it was almost ludicrous the way in which the fear slipped away and a look of heart-felt relief flashed on to the man's face. Removing the star from his shirt, he handed it over to the business man who took it and pinned it in turn on Bret's shirt.

'We're might proud to have you with us, Mr Manders,' he said quietly. 'I think, in fact I'm sure, there's going to be a bright future for Sundown now. We'll have a discussion tomorrow about that.'

After they had gone, with Veldon waddling behind them, Bret stood by the window and stared out into the bright sunlight. Life was strange, he mused, and there were so many odd twisted paths through it that a man had to have a sense of humour to face up to it at times. He fingered the silver star on his shirt, then tightened his gunbelt and walked out on to the street.